The Ghosts of Blackbottle Rock

Martyn Beardsley

T0306437

OUR STREET BOOKS

Winchester, UK
Washington, USA

First published by Our Street Books, 2017
Our Street Books is an imprint of John Hunt Publishing Ltd., Laurel House, Station Approach,
Alresford, Hants, SO24 9JH, UK
office1@jhpbooks.net
www.johnhuntpublishing.com
www.ourstreet-books.com

For distributor details and how to order please visit the 'Ordering' section on our website.

Text copyright: Martyn Beardsley 2016

ISBN: 978 1 78535 615 5
978 1 78535 616 2 (ebook)
Library of Congress Control Number: 2016954754

All rights reserved. Except for brief quotations in critical articles or reviews, no part of this book may be reproduced in any manner without prior written permission from the publishers.

The rights of Martyn Beardsley as author have been asserted in accordance with the Copyright, Designs and Patents Act 1988.

A CIP catalogue record for this book is available from the British Library.

Design: Stuart Davies

Printed and bound by CPI Group (UK) Ltd, Croydon, CR0 4YY, UK

We operate a distinctive and ethical publishing philosophy in all areas of our business, from our global network of authors to production and worldwide distribution.

The Ghosts of Blackbottle Rock

Author's Note

Polruan is a real place in Cornwall, and if you ever visit you will be able to follow in the footsteps of Charlie, Wei-Li and Mohan. Most of the places mentioned are to be found in Polruan and Fowey, but in some cases I have changed the name. 'Treffry House', for example, is actually Place House, the ancient home of the Treffry family. All of the characters in the story, however, are the product of my imagination. In particular, I'm sure the owner of the real gift shop isn't even slightly creepy! And there isn't a haunted house on West Street – as far as I know…

one

Charlie knew the Witch was watching his every move. Watching, waiting. Plotting to destroy him. Sitting at the back of the little ferry as it chugged and bobbed through the water from Fowey on its way to Polruan, he knew she would be able to see him directly from her lair right now. The orange and white boat nudged against the stone steps of the quay and people began to stand, ready to disembark. Charlie rose too, clutching a rail to keep his balance while the ferryman hauled on a rope to secure the vessel to a rusty metal ring bolted to one of the steps.

It felt as though she was trying to pull his gaze in her direction: to the old fisherman's house, now a holiday cottage nestling at the end of a short, gloomy alley at the back of the quay where the sun's rays never reached. He resisted. The showdown would come soon enough. He clambered over the side of the ferry and trudged up the steps, focusing only on the backs of the tourists in front of him.

Now came the hard part. Charlie's legs dragged stiffly and reluctantly; his heart felt heavy like black smog. But he had to go through with it. He walked along the busy little quay, weaving among the dawdling sightseers and tightly parked cars. Heading for the Witch's lair.

Passing from the warm Cornish sunlight into the shady coolness of the alley, Charlie soon saw that the door was ajar. Of course. Much as he had put this moment off, she knew he had to come sooner or later. Was he in fact entering now of his own free will, or had the Witch planted something in his mind that had made him do it? Charlie didn't know. He didn't seem to know anything for sure any more – except that he had to get this over with. He hesitated, then pushed against the door and was swallowed by the darkness of the interior. Surrounded as it was by tightly packed cottages, very little natural daylight reached this ground floor room. Without a light on, and while his eyes still struggled to readjust, it was hard to tell whether there was even anyone in here with him. He edged forward cautiously. There was a step where the reception area became an open-plan kitchen, and he felt for it tentatively with his foot.

Then he heard the faintest of creaks, and he knew he wasn't alone. Charlie couldn't so much hear her breathing as *sense* it.

By now, his eyes were used to the lack of light and he could see right to the back of the kitchen. There was no one there. Yet it continued – the faintest whisper of breath in the air.

'*Charlie…*'

He sprang back, startled, confused.

'*Charlie, come here.*'

Her voice was coming from above him. Then he remembered the layout of this place – he had walked past a central wooden-railed stairway on his left, which twisted up to the next floor. She must be up there, looking down at him. He turned to face her.

'*Why can't you leave me alone*? You've already trapped my dad. Why do you need me as well?' He was surprised by how strong and confident his own voice sounded. It boosted his morale.

'I haven't trapped anyone, Charlie. Your father wants to be with me. I only want you and me to be friends…'

Her voice was gentle, quiet, almost pleading – a tone he'd never heard from her before. But it didn't fool him for a minute. 'You're just mad because I'm not a pushover like he was! He was so lonely after Mum died he would have been taken in by *anybody's* smooth talking.'

Charlie suddenly darted up the stairs. He brushed past her, past the first floor and the sound of the TV coming from the room where he knew his father would be, and on to the next level and his own bedroom. He slammed the door behind him and sank down on the edge of his bed, planting his elbows on his knees and flopping his chin so heavily into his cupped hands that his teeth clicked unexpectedly and painfully together. He didn't care.

He didn't care if he'd broken all his teeth. He didn't care about *anything*. Looking out through his window over the roofs of the holiday cottages, he could see Polruan harbour below. The end of the Fowey River estuary was on the left, opening out to the sea. The backs of other holiday cottages and the storeroom of the Beachcomber, the gift shop on the quay, faced him. And that was it. Two pubs, one tiny general store, an even tinier café. That was Polruan – and they thought he would enjoy it! There *were* exciting places in Cornwall, Charlie knew because he had visited them in the past, when Mum was alive. Places with amusement arcades, adventure parks with giant water flumes, golden beaches where you could go body-boarding. This wasn't one of those places. And even if it had been, Charlie wasn't in the mood for it. Maybe if it had been just himself and Dad… The Witch spoiled everything – and it looked like she was here to stay. Everything was ruined forever.

A seagull flapped lazily past his window. Its size took him by surprise, and it mewed plaintively the way real gulls did, unlike the little scrawny little things squabbling over scraps in his home town. It landed on the chimney of a roof just below his window, where the houses sloped down Polruan's steep hill towards the river, and seemed to look at him with its beady yellow eyes. Charlie wished he had the gull's wings, its freedom just to launch itself into the sky whenever it wanted to get away and look down on all the stupid human activity below…

The sound of the doorknob turning snapped him back to reality.

'Charlie…'

His father sloped into the room, gently pulling the door to again. He was tall and angular in a slightly ungainly way; pain was etched into his normally kindly features and soft blue eyes, and Charlie couldn't ignore the glimmer of guilt he sensed behind the dark clouds of his own moodiness. He seemed to hate the whole stupid world these days – but if there was one exception it was Dad, who was in the same boat as him. Or would have been if the Witch hadn't come along.

'I know how difficult it's been for you…'

'No you don't.'

'I know it *has* been difficult. I can understand your feelings towards Sue—'

'No you can't.'

Dad sighed wearily.

'I think I can.' His voice was firmer now, and Charlie sensed he had better not push his luck too far. Dad was the king of laid-back, but he had learned two things about that. One was that when he *did* lose his temper, it was something wondrous and scary to behold (there had only been two times in Charlie's whole life, and he could remember both of them in vivid and awesome detail). There was never any physical violence or even the hint of it. It was far worse than that. The other point was – and there was no getting away from it – if you were such a dork that you made even the king of laid-back himself lose his temper, you must surely deserve everything you got.

'Did you know you've made Sue cry?'

As bad as things were, Charlie was shocked. He had never made an adult cry before. There was a weird feeling of power – but a much more awful, horrible guilt. His venomous words to her echoed in his ears, and now they didn't sound so clever. He had gone too far, and a braver kid than him would offer to apologise. But to his shame, it did occur to him that if he had upset her *that* much, maybe she actually would give in and leave them alone…

'Believe it or not, Charlie, she actually *likes* you.'

'No she—'

'She *does*! She understands – and don't say she doesn't! I know her and understand her better than anyone I've met in my whole life… Except Mum of course,' Dad added hastily. 'And she understands *you* better than you think. Her parents split up when she was eight, and she never saw or heard from her dad again.'

'Splitting up's not the same as someone dying.'

'No, but as far as it affected her life her dad might as well have been dead. She realises how hard it is for you to have a new woman coming into my life, and she would never pretend she could take the place of Mum. But she loves me and I love her, and we have to try to find a way to make this work. Please be patient, Chas; if not for her sake, then for mine.'

Charlie made a movement of his head which might have been a nod, but which wasn't distinct enough to be held against him in the future if he couldn't keep to it. Dad came over and hugged him. It was their first hug in quite a while, and Charlie suddenly found he didn't want to be let go of. He felt a funny tightness in his throat and a sting in his eyes when Dad pulled away with a ruffle of his hair and crept out of the room, but he quickly swallowed the feeling back before it engulfed him.

Charlie pulled up the old-fashioned wooden chair from beside his bed, tipping off his book, watch, and the sweaty T-shirt he'd meant to put in the wash days ago, and positioned the chair squarely in front of the window. Then he reached across and grabbed his binoculars from the dressing table and settled himself down to watch the boats cruising between the open sea and the sun-sparkled Fowey estuary. It was the only thing he derived any pleasure from in this place. He was fascinated by the locals pottering about in little boats as casually as people in cars and kids on bikes back home. He often watched the ferry motoring endlessly back and forth, transporting locals, bringing new batches of holidaymakers. He liked trying to identify the nationality of the flags of some of the more bigger and exotic boats that came in from time to time. And just occasionally he would spot the black-and-white pilot's boat heading out; he had come to realise that this heralded the arrival of a big container ship bringing a new cargo to the industrial port, just out of sight round the bend in the river beyond Fowey. These vessels were sometimes so long that they filled almost the whole window as they passed by, and the bridge was level with the upper floors of the houses on the opposite shore. The mighty blast from their horns echoed across the water and around the hills surrounding the amphitheatre-like estuary.

Another regular sight now caught his eye. Every so often, the man who ran the gift shop would traipse up the steps to a door at the back, pull out a bunch of keys, unlock it and disappear inside for a few minutes. Hardly exciting, but in a place like this almost anything that happened could seem interesting – and there was something creepy about him. He was a small, slightly built man, quite a bit older than Dad. He had a little upturned nose, a few strands of grey hair combed across his bald head, and wore thick-lensed glasses with heavy black frames. On this occasion the man left the door open when he went in, which was unusual. Charlie could see a trestle table with something on it: large, dark, rectangular, like some sort of box. Out of a combination of boredom and sheer nosiness, Charlie trained his binoculars in that direction and adjusted the focus. It was just some sort of big book with a stiff, plain cover and, judging by the yellowed edges of the pages, a very old one. The shopkeeper came back into view and, after checking outside that he was still undisturbed, he turned to the table and opened the book. He hunched over it, frowning, thumbing through as if searching for something in particular. This scene was being played out less than twenty metres below him, and thanks to his binoculars Charlie could see that the pages were filled with spidery handwriting divided into several columns, like some sort of register or accounts book. Then, the man seemed to find whatever it was he was looking for. He smoothed the page fully open, took off his glasses, breathed on them and wiped them. He almost pressed his pug nose into the book and stared at some particular entry for several minutes, as if it were a treasure map and he had found the X marking the spot. Finally, he slowly straightened up. He gazed into space for a time, and Charlie thought he detected a slight shake of the head. Then, without warning, he suddenly grasped the page he had been reading and tore it out.

Charlie was shocked. Even though he couldn't see what the book was, it looked somehow important, special – not the sort of historical volume people normally vandalised. The man folded the ripped-out page and put it in the back pocket of his trousers, slamming the book shut. He shuffled out of sight for a moment, and when he returned he had a plastic shopping bag. He placed the book in the bag, stuck his head out of the door to check that no one was about, then left the storeroom. He locked the door and set off with the concealed book under his arm.

Charlie sat back with a furrowed brow and let out a long breath. What on earth was *that* all about?

There was something weird about the little man, no doubt about it. Charlie didn't like the look of him – never had. But then, these days, Charlie didn't like the look of anyone.

two

The following day, Charlie had to tag along with Dad and the Witch, exploring the area.

Correction – *Sue.*

He had vowed to at least try to *think* of her less harshly, even if he couldn't – and had no intention of – making friends with her. She wasn't even the prettiest of the women Dad had met since Mum had died. The first time he saw her, Danny Lewis, his mate at school, had tried to make out she was the sexiest thing since Miss Amery who taught the Year Sevens. But then Sue had been wearing a top which showed her boobs a bit. Okay, she was quite curvy and had shiny, swishy dark hair and shiny, dazzly dark eyes. Things like that easily impressed Danny. Especially a glimpse of boobs. Charlie wasn't so easily impressed by appearances – and in this case he *refused* to be.

Dad and Sue hauled themselves up the lung-burningly steep hill out of the village, towards the coast and cliff-top footpath. The sun sparkled on sea as blue as in postcards, stretching out to the vast horizon, disturbed only by a distant boat with white sails leaving a trail of ripples in its wake. It was pretty breath- taking – but Charlie kept the thought to himself. They were looking for a specific location, which was one of the main reasons they'd come to Polruan. Sue was a writer, and she had plans to write a book about a supposedly famous shipwreck here. Something about a poor fisherman in a sinking boat being saved by a local hero, moving to London and going on to become a successful businessman. It was known as the Blackbottle Rock Disaster, because although the man who was saved had done well for himself, he hadn't been alone, and many others had drowned.

Charlie's pumping heart and rasping breath had just started to settled down from the climb, when they spotted a plain wooden bench just off the footpath. As they wandered along a grassy slope overlooking the sea, Dad looked up from his map.

'This is it! Blackbottle Rock is right beneath us.'

Below the field, Charlie could see jagged, pale grey rocks. At the bottom, there was a bigger and much darker, prominent rock with white waves gently washing over its base.

'It looks *nothing* like a black bottle.'

Dad shrugged. 'Maybe it does if you're on a ship at sea.'

'Lantic Bay…' Sue murmured distractedly, gazing down at the scene. 'Twenty-three died – eleven of them children. It's a lot of people – must have ripped the heart out of a little place like Polruan.'

'*At*-lantic Bay,' Charlie corrected her, triumphant at spotting her fault.

But Dad shoved the map under his nose. 'No, mate. *Lantic* Bay.'

'It's a misprint, then…'

'You'd think so,' said Sue in her usual infuriatingly understanding tone. 'But I've seen it on other maps too.'

She took some pictures and made notes in a little book, took one last wistful look down at the rock as if she could see the lifeless bodies being tossed and broken against its dark, unyielding presence, and then they turned back to explore Polruan itself.

'*Why* do we need to look round?' Charlie whined once they were back among the narrow streets and lanes, with weird names like Tinker's Hill and Betty Woons. 'We've been here four days – we know it's just a one-horse town!'

'There are lots of twisty little side-streets. It's interesting just to wander round old fishing villages,' Dad ventured.

'I always think it feels like going back in time when you lose yourself in quaint old places like this,' Sue added dreamily.

'It's not *big* enough to get lost in,' grunted Charlie.

'Yes,' said Dad – to Sue, not Charlie. 'Especially here. There are lots of lovely old villages in Britain, but Cornwall is, well…'

'*Cornwall*!' Sue finished the sentence for him.

Charlie grimaced as they gazed into each other's eyes and reached out to hold hands.

Oh, pleeeease…

'Look,' Sue said as they rounded a tight corner at the end of a row of cottages.

'Wow,' said Charlie. 'A shop! That makes *two*. I can hardly wait to write another postcard to Gran and tell her.'

'It's a sort of antiques shop!' said Dad. He loved old things. Sue *said* she did too, but Charlie suspected it was just because she knew Dad did.

After a couple of minutes poking around in the tiny shop, Charlie left them to it and wandered outside, smooching around with his hands in his pockets. An old man, bald, plump, face like a walnut but for his rosy-cheeks, came by walking a little white dog. He grinned at Charlie, but Charlie scowled and turned away. He was surprised anyone could live to that age in this place. How come they didn't all die of boredom before they were twenty-five?

Dad and Sue came out proudly clutching a parcel – he neither knew nor cared what it was. They ended up reaching the sea at a spot right on the edge of the village away from the houses, where there was an old ruined building like a castle, but little bigger than an ordinary house. Dad said it was called the Blockhouse. In the old days they used to have a chain slung across the floor of the river between here and a second blockhouse on the opposite side, and if enemy ships were spotted they could tighten the chain to stop them from getting into the harbour. Charlie had to admit – but not out loud – that there were some pretty spectacular views along the coast and out across the sea from the Blockhouse's windows.

They returned to the cottage for lunch. Dad did the evening meals when they didn't eat out, and Sue made the lunches. Charlie had told her what sort of stuff he liked – and she always came up with something that wasn't on his list. Hummus instead of ham. Wraps instead of sarnies. All sorts of weird stuff. And he always flipping well liked it. And he always made sure he left some and said he wasn't very keen on it, no matter how much his stomach begged him to finish it off. And she always smiled kindly and flashed those dazzly dark eyes at him, as if she could read his mind.

Witch.

Dad was busy unwrapping his new buy at the kitchen table while Sue chopped rapidly and expertly away at the organic bean sprouts or whatever fancy thing she'd come up with this time. Once Dad had cast aside the outer layer of blue wrapping paper and then the protective inner layer of newspaper, he held aloft a silver tankard of some sort as if it was the FA Cup itself.

'This was owned by an old Cornish fisherman – maybe he lived in this very cottage!'

'I'm not surprised he got rid of it – tatty old thing.'

Charlie was surprised to hear Sue's laughter. It was a natural laugh, not a forced one to prove she liked him. He hadn't meant it to be a joke. Well, maybe. Sort of. Now he had made her cry and laugh within the space of twenty-four hours. He wondered – if she had been the one who had made him cry yesterday, would he so gladly laugh at her jokes today?

In the next instant, Charlie was grabbed by the throat.

In a manner of speaking.

It was the headline on the crumpled front page of the local newspaper the tankard had been wrapped in:

Precious book stolen from Lanteglos Church

Charlie recognised the unusual name of the church from signs they passed in the lanes around Polruan, and he knew it was very close by. And he remembered the creepy gift shop man poring over the old book inside his storeroom. He knew the old book the Creep was furtively studying could have been anything – but Charlie had a gut feeling about it. And Charlie's gut feelings were usually right.

He snatched up the page. The report said that someone had broken into a locked cupboard and had taken one of the church's old parish registers containing records of nineteenth-century baptisms, weddings and burials. The police were puzzled, because the book was worth very little and was only of historical interest. Many, much more valuable, items had been ignored by the thieves.

Or 'thief', thought Charlie.

'Something interesting there, Chas?' Dad asked.

Sue appeared, humming a tune and putting plates on the table. Even though it was only a hum, he was surprised by how good her singing voice sounded.

'I'm not sure... I'll look at it later.' He folded the sheet of paper up and stuffed it into his pocket.

*

Why was it that when you really wanted to look at something through binoculars – *really* wanted to look – not only did they go all wobbly, but the lenses started to steam up? Charlie yanked up the bottom of his T-shirt and rubbed. There wasn't actually anything to look at as yet – the grey door to the mysterious room at the back of the Beachcomber was shut, and there had been no sign of the Creep in the hour or so that Charlie had been at his look-out post. But a spy had to put up with hours of boredom yet stay on the alert. He lay the binoculars in his lap to give his eyes a rest for a while. A minute later, a grey Royal Navy ship came gliding down the river. Several sailors in smart blue uniforms moved about the upper deck, and on the side, near the prow, it had *P714* marked out in bold letters. Charlie wondered what the 'P' stood for. He was interested in stuff like that, and had already learned that 'F' stood for frigate and 'M' was a minesweeper, but he hadn't come across a 'P' before. Maybe it stood for 'port', because, being small it was attached permanently to guard a particular port rather than sail the open seas. Or perhaps it could be… Charlie grabbed the bins.

There he was.

The Creep.

The little man pushed his dark-rimmed glasses, with their lenses like the bottom of Coke bottles, further up his piggy nose as he plodded up the steps to his storeroom. Just as before, he checked the coast was clear before unlocking the door; but this time, having opened it he went back down the steps to the car park on the quay. His expression never seemed to alter, like a mask – yet you could see from his darting eyes that his mind was working overtime, gnawing away at something. Within thirty seconds he was back, carrying something he must have removed from his car, which Charlie knew he always parked just outside the shop. This was suspicious enough – but it was what he was carrying that made things much more interesting. Charlie quickly raised the bins to his eyes.

Why was it that when you really wanted to see something through binoculars in a hurry, you never seemed to be able to line it up or even find it though the lenses? He pulled them away from his eyes, lined them up and tried again. He was just in time to see the Creep hauling not a suspicious book, but a long rolled-up rug.

The kind murderers in films used to hide bodies in.

And it looked heavy.

Charlie's heart put on a sudden spurt, and the binoculars began to shake in his hands, distorting the image.

No wonder the Creep was acting so strangely and making sure no one could see what he was up to…

Had someone discovered he was the precious parish register thief and he'd done away with them?

Charlie let out a shaky breath and adjusted the focus to see if he could make anything out inside the room, but it was just too dark. He scanned around, twiddling the focus knob again, but now it all looked different. Not darkness, but something blocking his view. Soon, he realised he had an extreme close-up of some sort of textile – the sort of stuff a jacket might be made out of…

He slowly scanned upwards. The Creep's face filled his field of vision, ice-blue eyes magnified by the thick lenses of glasses. *Staring right at him.*

Charlie gasped and let the binoculars drop as if they burned his hands. Now, their naked eyes met. Distantly, but definitely. And even though the Creep's expression never changed, Charlie picked up a gut-wrenching sense of fury, even hatred in that deep, burning gaze. Panicking, he slid down in the chair so he was below the level of the window – and as soon as he did so he could have kicked himself. If he had only stayed put and acted innocently, pretended to look at the boats out on the water, the brightly painted houses lining the Fowey side of the river, the seagulls. Anything. Then he might have brazened it out. To dive for cover was an admission of guilt. But who was he trying to kid? Their eyes had met. The Creep *knew* he was being spied on. The man who had probably murdered someone over a mouldy old church book *knew* that the boy in the holiday cottage behind his storeroom had discovered his secret. The next edition of the local paper flashed into his mind:

Young holidaymaker goes missing in Polruan

Slowly, cautiously, Charlie raised his head until his eyes were peeping above the window-ledge. The shopkeeper had gone. The grey door was shut.

But what was behind it?

And more to the point – where was the Creep headed?

three

'Anything to report from your look-out post, Charlie?'

He was vaguely aware that Sue was trying to make conversation. He had just come down to the first floor, where the main living area was because it was lighter and there was a view of the river; and to say the least, he was distracted. In fact, Charlie was actually shaking, though he did his best to hide it. He kept glancing over Sue's shoulder through the window to the narrow alley down which the Creep would have to come.

'Yes. Er…no, not really. Nothing interesting. Navy ship. What does 'P' stand for?' He blurted all this out quickly. All of Charlie's animosity and surliness towards her had been vaporised by shock and fear, and he had discovered a sudden desire to be a fully paid-up and warmly accepted member of the 'family'. If the Creep came looking for him, he wanted to be deep in conversation with Sue or Dad, acting perfectly naturally. He suddenly needed their protection. It was funny how having a killer on your case could instantly solve all sorts of relationship problems.

'What does 'P' stand for? I'm not sure what…'

'Navy ships always have a letter in front of their number. If you saw one with "F200" on it, the "F" would mean it was a frigate. "M100" would be a minesweeper,' he jabbered. 'They all have something like that. But I just saw one outside with a "P" on it. I've never seen one with a "P" on it before, and I was wondering if you knew what "P" stood for. I mean, it *could* be "Port", but I don't think…'

He trailed off, suddenly aware that Sue, and Dad behind her, was staring at him as if he had grown an extra head. Maybe his attempt at acting natural wasn't going too well. Maybe spewing out more words in thirty seconds than he had spoken to Sue in the last six months was over-doing it a bit. Maybe—

Charlie's eyes caught movement in the alley, and his legs

suddenly felt as if they were about to give way.

The Creep was coming this way…

'IT'S HIM!' he yelled, his voice almost breaking with panic.

Dad and Sue turned to the window, following Charlie's gaze. But the Creep had already passed out of sight.

'Who? Who's coming?'

'*Quick, call the police*!'

'Charlie, what's wrong, mate?' asked Dad.

He was about to explain – *try* to explain – when the knock came.

Charlie thought he was going to faint. There was a sickening, gurgling warmth in the pit of his stomach, and the room began to swim before his eyes. He wanted to tell them not to answer it, to pretend there was no one in. But by the time he had clutched the back of a chair, taken a deep breath and steadied himself, it was too late. Dad had gone downstairs, with Sue following close behind.

Charlie made his way to the stairs on wooden, unwilling legs. He crept halfway down, crouching, just in time to see through the bannisters Dad open the door to reveal the Creep: shifty eyes behind thick glasses, an aloof but polite smile on his face.

'Sorry to bother you, but I wonder if you might be the owner of a red Honda parked on the quay? It's blocking a delivery van.'

He was courteousness itself. But all the time his eyes were looking beyond Dad and into the cottage, searching…

'No, ours is a silver Ford.'

'Ah, of course! I remember seeing you about the place now. Where was it you said you were from?'

'I'm not sure we've ever spoken to be honest, but—'

Charlie wanted to scream *DON'T TELL HIM! DON'T TELL HIM ANYTHING ABOUT US!*

'—we're down from the Midlands. Long drive – but worth it!'

'Glad you like it.' He grinned, all full of mock friendliness. 'You have that nice little boy with you, don't you?'

'That's right.' Dad grinned back. 'Charlie!'

'Ah, yes. Charlie Thompson, wasn't it?'

'Er…no. Meadows, actually, but—'

'Oh, my mistake. Anyway, as I say – sorry to bother you.'

Without warning his eyes suddenly flicked upwards and locked on to Charlie's, almost as if he'd known he was there all along. It was just a split-second, but Charlie felt as though the Creep had reached into his soul and wrenched it out. And then he was gone.

'Strange bloke,' said Dad when they were all back together upstairs.

'He was fishing for information,' Sue agreed. 'Probably a holiday cottage salesman or something.'

Charlie stepped between them, trembling and pale. It was time to get it all out into the open.

'That man – the one who runs the Beachcomber…' The words came out jerkily, as if he had just run a marathon.

'Yes?'

'I think he's a murderer. Or thief – or *something*.'

Their faces were suddenly full of concern – but to his dismay Charlie knew in his heart that it was concern for his sanity, not his safety.

'Look, Charlie,' Dad said. 'I know that you feel excluded and that it's messing with your head, and—'

'No! This is *real*!' He explained about the old book and the body in the rug, and pulled out the page he had saved with report about the theft of the parish register.

'But lots of people own old books, Chas,' said Dad. 'And the body, well, you only caught a quick glimpse. You might have got it wrong…'

'I know what I saw!'

'Okay, okay. But things aren't always what they seem. He hardly looks like a master criminal, let alone a murderer. There could be any number of explanations.'

'Well you should have seen his face when he realised I'd seen what he was up to.'

'I dare say *I* wouldn't have been too pleased if I saw someone spying on me through binoculars!'

'But it *is* quite a coincidence,' Sue ventured. 'The bloke and the book, the newspaper article – *and* whatever it was in the rug.'

Charlie could almost see the wheels turning inside his dad's head: *I don't believe all this for a minute…but then maybe Sue doesn't…maybe she's trying to show support for Charlie and win him over…maybe I'd better at least seem to go along with it if only to back Sue up…*

'Well, you might have a point…'

Yaaay! Charlie didn't care whether they believed him or were pretending to believe him right then. He just needed them on his side, otherwise it was him alone against the Creep.

'But,' Dad added quickly, 'we can't go to the police just with that. They'd never believe us and we'd end up looking fools.'

'But we can't just ignore it either! What if I'm right? How would you feel if he struck again?' Charlie didn't add *and the victim was me*, but that's what he was thinking.

'You'll just have to keep spying on him, mate. Come up with some more evidence.'

This angered Charlie, because he knew for sure now that his dad was simply humouring him. He turned on his heels and marched up to his room.

The grey door was shut and there was no sign of the Creep. Charlie repositioned his chair so that he could no longer see it – or be seen from it. This had all become too much. If Dad didn't want to get involved, he certainly wasn't going to risk his neck alone. All he needed to do was keep his head down, stay out of the man's way for a few days. Then he could go home and forget about it.

Even the river seemed less fascinating now. He got his laptop from the table in the corner of the room, sat back down and fired it up. At least they had an internet connection here. Dad's phone, on a different network to his and Sue's, couldn't even find a signal, much to his annoyance. And they thought this was the best place in the world!

Once he'd booted the computer, he went into 'networks' the way Sue had shown him and selected the one he needed. (He had listened on in grumpy silence, grunting every now and then to show he understood, and ended by saying he'd probably never bother to go online anyway. He'd logged on at least twice a day since then.) His first job was to do a bit of googling and find out what the 'P' stood for on the side of Navy ships. That was harder than he thought – and he had to wade through loads of irrelevant American information before he finally got his answer. *Patrol Vessel*. Hmmm. Bit of an anti-climax. Then he logged into Gmail and saw he had new messages. There was one from Mike in Chicago. It would probably be the middle of the night there by now so that could wait. Another was from the devastatingly gorgeous Anna in Edinburgh who he'd met on some site or other and stayed in touch with. Why couldn't they have had a holiday in Edinburgh? And there were three from Danny, his mate at school. He was following a link from Danny to a whacky video on YouTube when he heard the brief jingle that alerted him to someone wanting to chat. His heart leapt. *The gorgeous Anna*?

No such luck. The username was one he didn't recognise: *Nemesis*.

Charlie didn't know what it meant, but somehow he didn't like the sound of it. Probably just because the Creep had spooked him. He sat transfixed for a moment by the blinking box in the bottom right-hand corner of the screen.

Nemesis

A little voice told him to delete it. Block it. Log off. He hovered the cursor over that last option, and his finger rested on left-click button of his touchpad. But curiosity won out over bad feeling. He had to know.

We have a problem, Charlie. You probably know that by now.

A hot, sick feeling washed through his insides. It was *him*. It had to be.

Who r u?

Nemesis

Who is Nemesis?

Someone who knows

How do u no who I am?

I am very clever, Charlie

How do u no I'm in trouble?

Charlie hastily deleted that – just stopping himself from sending it in time.

Problem? Dont no what yr talking abt

You will

Sod off. We've called the police!!!!!!!!

To his amazement, that did it. Nemesis vanished from the screen. Charlie was still feeling nauseous with fear, but that hasty retreat lifted his spirits a little. The Creep was rattled! Now, Charlie thought, maybe he was gaining the upper hand, and all he had to do was—

Beep!

Nemesis was back.

Charlie had been in the middle of googling the name. The first result he clicked on said it was from Greek mythology.

It was a term used to describe one's worst enemy.

Swallowing hard, he clicked on the message.

I'm coming…

four

The knock at the door made Charlie jump even though he had been expecting it – and even though he could see the dark uniforms of the police officers through the frosted glass rather than the short, neat outline of the Creep. Dad opened the door and ushered them in. One was a young woman with blonde hair tied in a short ponytail. She was pretty, and had a very friendly face, which Charlie at least found reassuring. The other one was quite short for a policeman, though powerfully built, with broad shoulders and a rugged face like a boxer's. That one seemed surprisingly old for a policeman. He had taken his hat off on entering the room, revealing short-cropped, thick grey hair and that sort of wrinkling and sagging under the chin and around the neck that older people have. After greeting the officers, Dad invited them upstairs to where Sue was waiting, and they duly followed as Charlie and his dad led the way.

'I'm PC Retallick, and this is my colleague WPC Hill,' announced the older man as they settled themselves on the settee. 'I've got to say that I'm more than a bit mystified by the call we got. You think a stalker is bothering your son?'

'Not exactly a stalker...' Dad tried to explain about what Charlie had seen from his window, and the ominous message.

'So your *son* is the stalker!'

The policewoman laughed, and PC Retallick obviously thought he was being clever. Charlie fumed inwardly.

'*Steve*!' admonished WPC Hill. 'You saw something that worried you, Charlie?'

Once again, he went through the story of the Creep ripping a page out of the old book and hiding the rug that looked like it had a body in it.

'Henry Penhale hid a dead body inside his shop?' asked Retallick incredulously.

So, he had a proper name. *Henry Penhale* sounded a lot less dangerous than *Nemesis*. But it also meant that they *knew* the Creep. He might have guessed. They were probably best pals in a small place like this. There was no way these two jokers were going to believe his story. 'Not his *shop*.' How hard could this be to understand? 'A storeroom at the back.'

'And you think seeing him tear a page out of something and carrying a rug – if that's what you saw…'

Charlie wanted to yell *OF COURSE THAT'S WHAT I SAW!* But there was no point.

'…proves that Henry Penhale – ' he exchanged grins with WPC Hill – 'is some sort of *murderer*?'

'He knows it doesn't *prove* it,' Sue interjected politely but firmly on Charlie's behalf.

'As soon as he saw me watching, he gave me a horrible look like someone caught out and came straight here – to *this house*,' Charlie explained.

'Did he come inside?' asked the young woman.

'Well, no…'

'Was there anything suspicious about his behaviour? Did he try to barge in, make any threats?'

'No… But then he contacted me on the internet. He said he was coming to get me!'

'He used his own name?' asked PC Retallick.

Charlie hadn't developed such an intense dislike even for Sue as quickly as he had for this prat. 'No! No one does. He used a screen name.'

'Then how do you know it was him, love?' Hill asked sympathetically.

'It had to be. It happened right after he caught me watching him, and he knew all about me and the fact that I was in danger.'

The two officers swapped glances once more. 'I'm going to have to be straight with you,' said Retallick. 'We can't go accusing people on that basis. It's not that I don't believe the lad, but it's just not grounds for accusing anyone of anything – especially serious crimes. But I'll tell you what I'll do. We're parked down on the quay, and we'll pop in and have a chat with Henry. We won't mention your lad's name or identify him in any way, obviously.'

'*He'll still know*!' said Charlie.

'Well, do you want us to talk to him or not?' The policeman's sharpness betraying his irritation.

'Yes. Please just have a word,' Charlie's dad said. He turned to Charlie. 'At least then he'll know the police are aware of…the situation, and that might be enough.'

'Spot on!' said Retallick. He jumped to his feet and snapped his notebook shut seemingly eager to leave.

Charlie folded his arms disconsolately and didn't get up to see them off. WPC Hill was the last out of the door, and she paused momentarily after the others had gone.

'You did the right thing, Charlie. If you really believed he might be up to no good, you're right to speak out. If we were Scotland Yard we'd probably have the facilities and the tech to track down who sent the message, but…'

Charlie managed a smile. 'I know. Thanks anyway.'

As soon as they had gone downstairs, he rushed in the opposite direction – up past his own bedroom and on to the wooden steps leading to the attic. Up there was a window which offered, if you craned your neck a bit, a narrow view of the front of the Beachcomber.

The Creep – Henry Penhale – was there, rearranging the beachwear, toys and souvenirs in baskets outside the shop. Like watching a film without the sound, Charlie observed as Retallick and Hill approach him. They shook hands, all smiles as if they were old mates, just as he'd imagined. The conversation lasted all of two minutes, with lots of 'Sorry-but-got-to-look-as-though-we're-doing-our-job' body language from the PC Retallick. They obviously didn't even ask to see the storeroom. The three parted company laughing – no doubt Retallick was cracking a joke about the daft kid in the holiday cottage.

And for the first time, a wave of doubt did sweep over Charlie. What if he *was* wrong? He had never seen Penhale laugh before and now he had, he looked, well, *normal*. Charlie had expected him to react shiftily, defensively. If he was guilty, he was a good actor.

Charlie heard the sound of an incoming message on his laptop downstairs and he felt his skin tingle coldly. He shot down the steps as fast as he could and checked the screen.

Nemesis

But Henry Penhale was still outside his shop – wasn't he?

Charlie scrambled up the steps once more. There he was. Sorting, tidying. Not a care in the world. Back to the laptop.

Nemesis

Charlie stared at the screen. *Nemesis wasn't the Creep*!

He clicked on the message.

Sorry about the last message from my friend. He's a bit of a fruitcake. But he was kind of right. We do know you have a problem, and we can help. Contact me, not Mohan if you're interested. Wei-Li.

So Nemesis could still be Penhale – but this person was calling Nemesis 'Mohan', which sounded like an Indian name, so Charlie felt sure he had got it wrong. He figured *he* would be the one who had cause to feel sorry before too long – *if* he admitted to his dad and Sue that he had at least half the story wrong, that was. And if he had got the Nemesis part wrong, what was to say he wasn't mistaken about what the Creep was up to? His thoughts whirled like clothes in a washing machine. *Wei-Li* sounded Chinese. But how could a Chinese person be the sister of an Indian one? Was *Wei-Li* a way of signing off, like *Bye for now*? Maybe, but he figured it was probably a name. Female, probably – and someone who somehow knew about his 'problem'. Had they seen Penhale up to something too? And if Wei-Li and her friend Mohan were suspicious about the Creep, might it mean there really was something to it?

How do you know about all this? How did you find me?

Many locals know the truth, but they refuse to face up to it. Mohan traced you – he's good at hacking and stuff. (Sorry!)

How can you help?

We are members of an organisation that has experience in these matters. Can't say more here. Need to talk face to face.

How would I find you?

Look out of your window.

What?

We can see you

Charlie felt a tingle on the back of his neck and became suspicious again. They were watching him the way he had been watching Henry Penhale? He didn't like the sound of this. Could it be a trap – Henry Penhale had an accomplice? It seemed unlikely. In all the TV shows and films, serial killers and other crazy creeps were always loners. Another message from Wei-Li came through.

Get your bins and look towards Fowey for a light going off and on

Bins? Ah! Binoculars. *Bloody hell, they could see right into his room*! Charlie instinctively looked around for some kind of hidden camera.

HOW DO YOU KNOW ABOUT MY BINS??!!

We have a powerful telescope and we've seen you using them. Look near the church for the light in the window

Charlie had noticed the church. It was one of the most prominent things on the Fowey side, and actually seemed like a peculiar cross between a church and a castle – an ordinary church tower surrounded by what looked like battlements.

Once he had trained his binoculars on the area around the church, he did indeed see a light flashing off and on inside one of the rooms of the 'castle' part of the church.

You are in the castle?

Not a castle! Treffry House. Can you come?

Now?

Yes. You can't tackle this alone, and every minute that passes places you in greater danger.

Charlie wished they hadn't said that. It brought back the shivers, and the evil expression on Penhale's face when he had realised Charlie was spying on him. And if Nemesis and Wei-Li really were part of some sort of major crime organisation, like maybe MI5 or Special Branch or something (and didn't they have to be to own a massive place like that?) then that was just what he needed. He'd like to see the local country bumpkin cops' faces when his new friends arrived flashing their MI5 badges.

It could be some sort of ambush, but it didn't feel like it and Charlie needed answers.

I'll get the next ferry.

five

It was early evening, and Charlie had an hour before dinner to make the five-minute trip across the river, meet the mysterious people who had been watching him and Penhale, and get back. He surprised by how quickly Polruan had become almost deserted now the shops had closed. His footsteps echoed off the walls of the cottages as he made his way along narrow East Street, and it seemed he had the village to himself.

But not quite.

He saw a little, wiry man opening the door of a house in the distance. Charlie instantly recognised the figure and the furtive way he seemed to do everything, including the anxious glance up the street before entering. Charlie instinctively froze – but he didn't sense he'd been spotted.

So now he knew where Henry Penhale lived. Charlie slowed his pace right down as he got closer to the old house. It was not painted white or some pastel colour like its neighbours. It was a shabby, grey stone building, and looked as though it had been there forever. Above the door was a weather-beaten wooden nameplate with faded lettering: *Rosebud.*

There was no still one about, so Charlie risked loitering there for a moment. The narrowness of the street meant that the houses were in almost perpetual darkness on the ground floor – but no light had come on in the living room, so maybe he had gone into the back or upstairs. And now, as he peered inside, it seemed that this perhaps wasn't the Creep's house after all. Apart from the furniture, there were no personal belongings inside or any other signs of habitation. And now he saw that there was a card in the window – something about holiday cottages and who to contact to rent it out. What was Penhale doing in an empty holiday home? And why hadn't he turned any lights on?

Then, Charlie did see a light – but it wasn't an ordinary room light. What had caught his eye was a yellow flickering and flitting against the glass of an attic window jutting out of the grey slate roof above. Penhale was lurking about with a torch in there.

Charlie sank back into the shadows of a gap between two houses. He had no way of knowing whether Penhale was looking out into the street. It was so quiet that Charlie could now actually hear the man moving about the attic room – the faint clump of footsteps on bare wooden floorboards. It was all very strange, but frustrating. He wasn't likely to discover anything by standing outside, and didn't want to get caught when Penhale emerged. And he had an appointment with Wei-Li. Reluctantly, he turned his back on *Rosebud* to resume his short walk to the ferry.

And that was when it all kicked off.

The scream was the most obvious thing, but then came the face.

The way it happened was first, a strangled cry: a mixture of shock and fear, barely human – but Charlie knew it belonged to Penhale. The thin beam of a torchlight arced wildly, followed by a clatter as if it had been dropped to the floor. Then running footsteps on echoing floorboards. Then a face at the window. A face that did not belong to Henry Penhale. A face that seemed barely human.

It shimmered in the glass like a projection or reflection for a moment, and then was gone – but the image stayed burned in Charlie's mind. A bearded man wearing a peaked cap that cast a shadow over his eyes but didn't hide them completely. They smouldered like the embers of a fire and Charlie caught, just for an instant, the glowering malevolence behind them.

It felt as if his skin was crawling with insects, and he wanted to run but was fixed to the spot. Even when he knew the face had gone, even when he heard the Creep running down the stairs and making for the front door, Charlie couldn't move, couldn't even think.

Henry Penhale came tumbling out of the house, slamming the

door behind him. He lurched up East Street with the stiff gait of someone not used to running. Charlie heard him utter a little whimper as he went. The only good thing was that the Creep had been in far too much of a state to notice him.

His heart was still racing, but seeing Penhale disappear somehow broke the spell. Charlie took a last look at the attic window. Dark, plain, ordinary. As if nothing had ever happened.

But it had.

A face from a TV screen inside the room? A reflection from the opposite side of the street? It had looked somehow distorted: not just with rage, but physically rippling. It was an old house – maybe the small panes of glass were uneven like ones he'd seen in ancient stately homes. Maybe there was another explanation…

Then, something brushed against the back his leg. Charlie spun round and his involuntary cry reverberated along the street. A black cat slunk away, pausing to glance back at him through disdainful green eyes before disappearing down an alleyway. Charlie cursed it under his breath and hurried to the ferry.

*

As the boat backed away from quay, the sun was merging with the hills that surrounded the estuary. Soft low rays illuminated the river, and the glooping and slopping sounds the water made against the sides of the little orange ferry were strangely comforting. It was another world entirely to the dark and bizarre one Charlie had just left behind on East Street.

After that performance, he couldn't wait to see what these two strangers had to say about Henry Penhale. For all he knew, he might even be safely under the protective wing of two MI5 officers. He just hoped it was Wei-Li he would have to deal with, rather than Nemesis. Okay, his name was really Mohan. Charlie knew a Mohan, an Indian lad at school who was nice and quiet.

But there was something about the whole Nemesis thing that had left him harbouring a deep distrust and suspicion of this man, whoever he was.

The ferry picked a path between moored boats – mostly little ones, but a few impressive larger yachts swung at anchor here and there. They passed a cormorant perched on a huge buoy, spreading its wings out to dry in the last rays of the sun, and the man sitting next to him – the only other passenger – whipped out his phone to snap it. On Charlie's left, the river mouth opened out to the sea: a flat, dark expanse today blending into the darkening blue of the far horizon. It almost invited you to head out and explore it, and Charlie could understand why sailors in the old days couldn't resist the temptation to do just that. He already knew this was a trip the older Polruan kids made every day to a school in Fowey, and he thought of his own dreary bus-ride and wondered if they realised how lucky they were.

Within a few minutes, they had reached the Fowey landing. The old ferryman skilfully guided the boat until it gently bumped against the stone steps, then slipped from his seat at the steering wheel and deftly threaded the thick mooring rope through a metal ring on the harbour. He hauled on it with all his might to bring the vessel tight against the steps.

Charlie stood up early to be first off. Copying some of the locals he had noticed on previous trips, he nipped up the steps inside the boat and hopped across to dry land even while the ferryman was finishing securing the boat. He emerged at the top of the steps on the Town Quay. Fowey was quite a bit bigger than Polruan, and was still peppered with tourists and noisy seagulls looking for opportunities to steal chips and ice cream cones. Charlie had walked past the churchyard before, so he knew the direction to take from here. Within seconds, he had emerged into the tight and twisty main road, which ran through Fowey.

When the shops were open there usually seemed to be a throng like a crowd leaving a football match, spilling off the tiny pavements and into the road. Cars and delivery vans had to nose their way carefully through the ambling tourists with their cameras, babies in pushchairs, and carrier bags full of purchases. But now in the twilight it was much quieter, and Charlie was soon outside the church. The problem was where to go from here.

He had never quite been able to figure out the layout of this church-cum-castle. Were they all one building? From afar it looked like it – but now he was close up he could only see the church. Surely you didn't go through the church part to get to the castle? There was a side door to the church on his right – but something told him to skirt the churchyard along a narrow lane that ran uphill. A few metres further up was a turning to the right – and the entrance to the castle. *Treffry House*, as he now remembered Wei-Li had called it. And now he saw that they were two completely separate buildings which just happened to be next door to each other and made of what – from a distance at least – looked like a similar type and colour of stone.

Charlie hovered at the tall open gates, which led to the entrance to Treffry House. In a courtyard at the end of a drive of tiny loose pebbles he could see two people: a Chinese-looking man in a very smart suit and tie, and a woman emerging from what looked like a kitchen door carrying a large cardboard box. She handed the box to the man, who loaded it into the back of a big, gleaming four-wheel-drive car. If they were Nemesis and Wei-Li, they didn't betray any signs of recognising him. And now Charlie was confused. He'd convinced himself that Wei-Li was a woman, but the woman here was white European. And neither of them was Indian, like the Mohan he knew at school.

But then that was probably a secret agent thing. If you gave yourselves names that made no sense, it would make it that much harder for an enemy who was intercepting your messages to actually identify you in person. Clever. He stepped hesitantly towards two people.

'I'll be back around nine,' the man was saying in a refined but heavily accented voice. 'Make sure she has her meal at seven prompt, and don't stand for any nonsense about carrots. They *are* good for you.'

The woman laughed. '*You* can't get her to eat them, so what chance do I stand? She was older than Sue; tall and willowy, with lots of ethnic jewellery around her wrists and neck. Her accent sounded local. It was beginning to dawn on Charlie that these two might not be agents called Wei-Li and Mohan, unless they were putting on a really good act.

Had someone played a trick on him? Were they watching from somewhere, sniggering as he made a fool of himself? But he was committed now and continued to approach, his feet scrunching loudly on the driveway. The man had already jumped into the car and was starting the engine. The woman was striding gracefully towards a side door of the main building, but finally noticed him.

'Yes?'

'Er… I'm looking for…' Should he use the name? Was it some sort of code name that only he was supposed to know? There was no choice – what else could he say? 'Er, is this where Wei-Li…'

'*Ah*! Just through those double-doors, up the stairs and along the landing to the left. Look for the door that says, *No Entrance – Authorised Operatives only*. Something mysterious like that, anyway!' She laughed lightly almost to herself, then strode off through the side door.

Authorised Operatives! So there *was* some kind of government agency based here. But where did this man and woman fit into it, and why did they seem so unconcerned about who they allowed inside? Shouldn't there be security guards and doors that required swipe cards or fingerprint recognition to gain entrance? Or had they been keeping him under surveillance for so long that they knew exactly who he was and so weren't in the least worried by his arrival? Perhaps in a place like this there *was* tight security but it was well hidden to make the place look normal. It only swung into action if there was a potential threat…

The house was as big as a hotel, but eerily empty and quiet. Charlie found himself in some sort of dimly lit hallway. There was a room opposite with double glass doors, and a big picture window on the far side. Through it, and standing out vividly in the low lighting, he could see the river still sparkling in the rays of the sinking sun, and the bright colours of the boats. He headed up the thickly carpeted stairway, which broadened out at the top and circled round both to the right and left like stairs in stately homes – which he supposed this was. He turned to the left as instructed and found himself going up another shorter flight of steps. There were weird abstract paintings on the walls: angular shapes, which may or may not have been human, and angry slashes of reds and purples which Charlie couldn't decipher but found kind of unsettling. In contrast, a large stone Buddha sat serenely on a three-legged table in a corner of the smaller landing at the bottom of the final flight of stairs. And then he was at the top, looking along a long corridor also like those in hotels, with various doors of dark wood and polished brass knobs all along it. But he could only see one bearing any kind of sign, and as he made his way towards it he soon saw that it was the one he wanted. There were low voices coming from within, but it was a big, heavy door and he couldn't make out the words. He knocked, but there was no response and the voices continued. The *No Entrance – Authorised Operatives Only* sign seemed to stare down at him disapprovingly, but he knocked again. And when there was still no sign that anyone had heard, he gingerly opened the door. The voices ceased abruptly. Charlie hesitated, then stepped across the threshold. What he saw only added to his confusion.

Kids. There were just two kids. One was only about ten, of Asian appearance. He wore dark-framed glasses and was dressed like a fifty-year-old who thought jeans were too daring. He was sitting at a desk, the blueish light from a computer screen bathing his brown face and reflecting in the lenses of his spectacles. He glanced up at Charlie momentarily then returned to his screen, pushing his glasses further up his nose before commencing to jab rapidly and fluently at his keyboard. The other occupant of the room was a girl who appeared to be around Charlie's age – maybe twelve or thirteen. She looked Chinese and was sitting in a large, comfy armchair by a window, the sunlight illuminating her shoulder-length black hair and trendy purple top like a stage spotlight. Beside her was a telescope, pointing out towards Polruan.

Oh – and the girl was stunningly, impossibly beautiful.

She had the most exquisite, petite, doll-like features Charlie had ever seen. The gorgeous Anna from Edinburgh paled into insignificance beside her (although admittedly she was at something of an unfair disadvantage, since Charlie had only ever seen her in a rather dodgy digital photo).

'Hi!' said the girl brightly, springing lightly from her chair and walking over to him. Her rose petal cheeks glowed and her midnight-black eyes twinkled, and he felt something inside going all gooey.

'Hi…' But then Charlie remembered why he was here, and managed to snap himself out of the spell. He twisted his head back to double-check the sign on the door, and there was no mistake. This was supposed to be where the *Authorised Operatives* were to be found.

'But…you're *kids*!'

'Try getting an adult to believe your story,' said the boy at the computer curtly, not looking away from his monitor.

'I have,' Charlie faltered.

'Exactly.'

'Take no notice of him,' the girl said breezily. There was just a faint Chinese undertone to what otherwise sounded like 'standard English' accent. 'We're glad you came! Come and sit down, and I'll explain everything.'

She waved him over to the big chair she'd been sitting in, and since there was no other seat she nimbly swung herself up onto a table, shoving some paperwork aside to make room, and assumed a cross-legged position.

'The boy who probably gave you a bit of a fright earlier on is Mohan, sometimes known as The Geek. Because that pretty much sums up what he is.'

Charlie heard Mohan snort derisively, still not deigning to avert his gaze from his work. He was beginning to wonder whether coming here had been a big mistake.

'Look, it'll be dark soon and I can't stay too long. I really need to discuss this thing with you.' They might be kids, but at least they seemed confident, like people who knew what they were doing. 'What information have you got on him? Is he dangerous? What's he up to?'

Mohan stopped typing and finally turned to Charlie. 'We've been aware of him for a long time. There are still some gaps in our knowledge, but we think we have all the information we need in order to finally get rid of him.'

Charlie had never heard someone so young sound so self-assured and grown-up. But – *get rid* of him? 'I don't know about that. I mean, I might even be wrong—'

'Oh, no,' said Wei-Li. 'Your suspicions are right. You must be sensitive.'

'Well, I have become a bit touchy I suppose. But before Dad's new woman came along—'

'No, Charlie – I mean sensitive as in *psychic*. Like me!'

'Oh. Er…'

If she's psychic, does that mean she can read my thoughts? Does she know I fancy her?

Charlie felt himself blushing, studying her face carefully for any signs that she was searching his soul. He also decided to try to think only of football when he looked her way from now on.

'My main skill is to be able to communicate with those who

have passed over,' she added.

God, this is weird…

'Anyway,' said Mohan, picking up the story again. 'He has been up to his tricks in Polruan for quite some time, although few locals will admit it openly. He was born in 1815—'

'Whaaat?'

'—and he was a merchant of some sort. I haven't found out what sort exactly, but anyway he made money by buying and selling things—'

'*Whoah*!' Charlie cried. '*Eighteen-fifteen*? What the hell's going on here? Who *are* you people?'

'Oh, I should have said,' Wei-Li replied. 'We are Fowey Paranormal Investigations. We have known for years that the house you are staying in is haunted – several others are in Polruan – but you are the first person we've been able to convince. We can help your ghost to walk into the light – we've done it before with others!'

'*Ghost*? What about Henry Penhale?'

'Henry Penhale?' Wei-Li and Mohan asked in unison.

Charlie thought about the initials of the name of their group, and the penny suddenly dropped. 'Fowey Paranormal Investigations – the *FPI*! *Oh, pleeease*! One talks to dead people, and what does the other do?' Charlie demanded, looking Mohan's way. 'Catch vampires? My life is in danger from a possible murderer and all I get is a pair of nutters!'

He launched himself out of the chair and strode towards the door.

Wei-Li's voice stopped Charlie in his tracks. What she said in her calm, quiet, kindly voice, froze him to the spot.

'Your mother says she loves the pink angel.'

He stood with his back to the room, unable to turn and face her for a moment. He swallowed hard at the lump, which had filled his throat, and blinked away the stinging tears that swam before his eyes and threatened to spill down his cheeks.

He had put a little pink angel by the tree where his mum's ashes had been scattered. He was only six then, and it was just a cheap, plastic thing he'd seen in a toyshop. But it was his choice. His own innocent little gift to her. And whenever he had since visited the tree and seen that angel, it had always felt that Mum was close by. Really. Not like a memory, but *really*…

'She likes Sue. She's glad your father is happy again… She hopes you can be too.'

'Stop it!' he cried, spinning round. *'Don't make things up like that. It's cruel.'* He was so choked that could hardly get the words out, and he knew she could not possibly be making them up. It was too much. Charlie's strength failed him without warning and he crumpled, sobbing. It had been a long time coming, and it was almost a relief now that it had.

He felt Wei-Li's arm around his shoulders, soothing, like a cloak of comfort that kept out the bad and kept in the good. She led him gently back to the chair and sat him down.

'Forget the ghost,' she whispered. 'I'm sorry we got it so wrong. It seems you have a much more serious danger to face, and we have the skills to help you. We *will* help you.'

six

'Tell us about this man,' Wei-Li quietly urged. Charlie was back in the embrace of the big leather armchair and she was on the floor in front of him with her legs folded beneath her, sitting on her heels. The nearness of those profoundly dark eyes looking up at him was both comforting and slightly disconcerting. Even Mohan now seemed interested in the story he was about to hear and sat sideways in his chair, looking on intently.

Charlie told them about how shifty the Creep had seemed, how he had seen him tearing the page out of the old book and had then found out about the stolen parish register.

Mohan instantly swivelled back to his computer. 'I read something about that...'

'It was taken from Lanteglos Church,' Charlie told him. 'I found it by accident in an old newspaper.'

'Yes – here it is... Something odd about it. The thief or thieves ignored stuff that was worth a lot of money.'

'So they had a specific reason for wanting the register,' Wei-Li chipped in.

'Not "they",' Charlie insisted. '*Him*. I just know it. There is a particular baptism, marriage or burial that's important to him.'

'We can be more specific than that,' said Mohan, still studying the online accounts.

'What do you mean?' Charlie asked.

'Deaths or burials, that's what he was interested in. Parish registers do record baptisms and marriages as well – but the stolen book was just a burial register. It covered the years...let me see...1839 to 1863.'

'But you said something about a *killer*, not thief,' Wei-Li said.

'I was coming to that. Not long afterwards, I saw him hiding a rolled up rug in the storeroom of his shop...'

'And?' Mohan prompted him bluntly.

'And it looked heavy, as if it had a body in it.'

'But you didn't see a body? Feet sticking out? Trail of blood?'

'No, but...'

The more Charlie thought about it – what he had actually seen as opposed to what he suspected – the less certain he became in his own conclusions.

'Big rugs are pretty heavy anyway,' Wei-Li suggested sympathetically.

Mohan, who had been rattling away on the keyboard again, announced that there had been no reports of missing people or murders in the area for years.

"Well all right, maybe the body in the rug was my imagination. The Creep had me spooked by that time. *But* he was definitely acting suspiciously even then – he didn't want people to see what he was up to.'

'Maybe he's just one of these strange people who feel the need to steal random things,' said Mohan. 'Some weirdoes steal clothes they don't need from washing lines. Some people shoplift little items yet they're rich enough to be able to buy the whole shop.'

'But *Henry Penhale...*' Wei-Li mused. 'I mean, he's well known around here.'

'And much further afield,' Mohan added. 'A very respected figure. Very popular. Local historian, writes articles for magazines, gives talks on the radio.'

That got Charlie's hackles up. 'Doesn't mean he's a saint.' He glanced out of the window and saw the blue skies darkening. 'I've got to go now. Thanks for offering to help – but it's not up to me to find out who stole the burials register. And if Penhale's *isn't* a murderer, well, all the rest is someone else's problem. I hope you catch your ghost – but I haven't seen one where we're staying.'

It was only then that Charlie remembered the face at the window on East Street. For a second, he felt a chill run through him – but quickly dismissed it. No murderers, no ghosts. Forget it.

Wei-Li showed him to the door and stepped out into the corridor with him. 'I hope you enjoy the rest of your stay in Polruan.'

'I doubt it.' He realised how grumpy he must sound. 'But thanks…'

'And what I said about your mother was true. Bye, Charlie.'

She kissed him on the cheek and went back inside.

*

As Charlie sat on the ferry watching the first stars appear above the hills that surrounded Polruan and Fowey, he could still feel the warm glow on his right cheek where Wei-Li had kissed him…

The tempting smell of dinner greeted him as soon as he opened the cottage door. So much had happened today that he didn't have the energy to be angry with Sue, and when she made a friendly enquiry as to what he'd been up to, rather than being irritated by her nosiness he responded casually without really thinking.

'Made a couple of new friends in Fowey.'

'That's good!'

'You know that big castle thing next to the church?'

'Treffry House, yes.'

'Well, they live there. Or at least one of them does.'

'Wow!' Dad cried. 'You've been inside Treffry House?'

'Yep.'

It took him a while to build up to it, but later, when he was helping Dad to clear the dinner table, Charlie asked as insouciantly as possible, 'Do you believe in ghosts?'

'Nah! Load of rubbish.'

'I do,' said Sue, still sitting at the table.

Dad seemed thrown for a moment. He was so used to being in

tune with her and them agreeing on everything. 'Oh...well...I suppose anything's possible, but...'

Sue remained unperturbed. 'I saw one three years ago. I was in a library, researching for an article on local men who fought at Waterloo. There was a man with old-fashioned whiskers and a bushy moustache sitting in a chair the far a corner of the room, just staring into space. I thought he was odd, but I just tried to ignore him. He seemed perfectly real and solid. When I was leaving I saw a little display on the wall. The library had once been the private home of a rich businessman and there was a picture of him – the man I'd seen in the corner!'

Did you go back to see if he was there?' Charlie asked.

'I should have done, but that's grown-ups for you. We think we have to act "sensibly" and lose our sense of adventure. I bet you would have gone back to check!'

The face at the attic window flashed into his mind.

'Maybe...'

seven

Charlie had a choice to make. Go with Dad to a garage ten miles away to investigate a funny noise he thought the car was making (Dad was always claiming to hear funny noises, and they always turned out to be in his imagination) or traipse around Polruan with Sue while she carried out research on the story of the Blackbottle Rock disaster for her book.

No contest.

The trip to the garage would be boring, especially waiting around while mechanics looked under the bonnet and scratched their heads, but there was no way he was going to spend hours on his own with Sue.

No way, that was, until her heard more about her plans.

They had just washed up after breakfast. Sue was putting notebooks and stuff in a bag; Dad was pulling his trainers on.

'You must have heard it. It was like a *whee-whee-whee* sound whenever we dropped below thirty miles an hour.'

'Perhaps a little piggy got stuck under the bonnet,' Sue suggested, pinching his cheek, 'and it keeps going *whee-whee-whee* all the way home!'

Charlie stifled a giggle.

'Very funny. You'll both be laughing when we break down in the middle Bodmin Moor and the mists come down and we hear the mournful cry of the Hound of the Baskervilles getting ever closer.'

'That was Dartmoor,' Sue said, slinging her bag over her shoulder.

'Well, he's moved. Hounds do.'

'Sure you want to put up with that all morning rather than wander round in the sun with me?' Sue asked Charlie before she left. 'I'm meeting a man on the quay who knows about the Blackbottle Rock disaster. We're hiring a boat to take us out to the spot where the hero performed his gallant rescue.'

Charlie hadn't known about this boat trip and it captured his imagination – but he made sure his features remained impassive and merely shook his head.

Did she look a little hurt? Maybe. He felt a pang of remorse, but this was how it had to be and he pushed it away.

She shrugged. 'I'll just have to meet Mr Penhale on my own, then.'

Charlie had been about to head upstairs to grab his phone. He stopped in his tracks and spun round. '*What?*'

'Henry Penhale, the local history expert who's going to show me where the Rosebud sank and tell me the whole story. The few survivors owed their life to the courage of his ancestor.'

'But that's *him*!'

'Who?' asked Dad.

'The man who…' Charlie hesitated, remembering what a fool he'd made of himself only a couple of days previously. 'He's the one who came to the door on Monday…'

'Ah, the mass murderer,' said Dad, munching on a biscuit.

'Yeah, well… Anyway, he seems, er, interesting,' Charlie said, addressing Sue. 'And I didn't realise you were going on a boat. Is it all right if I go with you after all?'

Her face brightened. 'All aboard!'

*

As they waited at the appointed meeting place in Crumpets, the little teashop just round the corner from where they were staying, Charlie began to fidget nervously. He was trying to remember why he'd been so keen to come in the first place. Yes, there was still something decidedly peculiar, even suspicious, about the Creep; yes, he would love to know what was behind it. But there was nothing he could actually do. He'd *like* to ask him why he was ripping pages out of old books and lurking about in empty houses – and especially what gave him such a fright. But that wasn't going to happen, so not only was he stuck with Sue for ages, but wasting his time. All that would happen was that Penhale would recognise him as the boy who was spying on him through binoculars. Then again, he probably wouldn't bring it up with Sue being there.

Charlie's heart lurched when a new customer darkened the open Crumpets' doorway. Even without looking he somehow knew who it was and tried to avoid making eye contact for as long as possible. Which wasn't long.

'Ah, we meet again!'

Henry Penhale had a sort of tight-lipped smile that seemed more a matter of duty than genuine warmth. Sue rose and shook the pudgy hand he offered, and Charlie did likewise. He squirmed inwardly at the Creep's warm, slightly sweaty grasp. Once they'd settled themselves at the table, he was close enough to see that the strands of hair carefully plastered over his otherwise bald head weren't completely grey but had a sandy colour mixed in with it. The light above his head made the pink parts of his scalp gleam, and the whole arrangement just looked ridiculous.

'It's very kind of you,' said Sue. 'I hope you won't be losing any business in your shop because of this little jaunt.'

'Not at all. I have a part-time helper and she's in charge for the day.'

'Good. I'm looking forward to finding out all about what happened all those years ago.'

'Well,' said Penhale after they'd ordered drinks, 'nice day for a boat trip!'

'As long as we don't suffer the same fate as the boat that sank off Blackbottle Rock.' Sue smiled.

Charlie shuddered. Sailing out of the estuary into the open sea was the thing he'd been looking forward to the most. He hadn't quite connected it with the idea of visiting the place where people had drowned doing exactly the same thing.

'Not to worry, my dear. I've been out there countless times, taking people on my guided tours. It was an unusual combination of things that caused the boat to sink back in Victorian times: a freak storm, a sudden change of wind direction, and...' He trailed off quickly, and it struck Charlie that he'd just managed to stop himself saying something he preferred to keep to himself.

'What else?' he couldn't help asking.

'I beg your pardon?'

'You said the storm, the wind – and something else.'

Charlie noticed the briefest flash of anger in the pale green eyes, distorted by the thick lenses of his glasses. But he quickly resumed his smarmy smile.

'Oh, nautical things. I'm no sailor – that's why I get someone else to pilot the boat when I go out there.'

'Did you find the owner of the car?' Sue asked, changing tack abruptly.

'Car?'

'When we last met, you were trying to find the owner of a car causing an obstruction outside your shop.'

'Oh, *that* car...'

Although Charlie was sure he was trying to hide it, Penhale seemed surprisingly flustered by such a routine question. He also suspected that Sue had asked it as a kind of test...

'Yes, blocking the shop doorway – soon found him.'

'Ah, good. I could have sworn you said he was blocking a delivery van in but that must be me and my terrible memory!'

Penhale still seemed flustered and glanced down at his watch. 'Goodness me – the boat will be here any minute.'

They quickly finished their drinks and made their way down the short but extremely steep road to the harbour, with its usual mix of sightseers and ferry passengers milling around. Out on the river, a boat with a crew of four bustling about the deck in bulky lifejackets was progressing in a stately manner out of the estuary towards the sea. Despite the Creep's reassurances, Charlie was glad to see that it was a calm sunny morning. The waters around the coast were going to be as safe as could be.

A little blue and white boat with *Water Taxi* marked on it chugged into view and moored behind the Polruan ferry. As soon as the latter departed, the water taxi nudged forwards into its spot and Penhale led them down the steps. He greeted the man at the helm, and soon they were on their way. It seemed strange and even a little daunting to be heading for the open sea rather than the short, cosy trip to Fowey in the opposite direction. As the boat nosed round the corner of the quay, bobbing a little on the cross-current where river met sea, the river mouth opened out and Charlie's breath was taken away by the seemingly limitless body of water opening out before him. In the bright sunlight, it looked as if it had diamonds scattered on its surface. The boat puttered along at a sedate pace, and while they skirted the cliffs that sheltered Polruan on the other side, Henry Penhale began to explain what had happened here over a hundred and fifty years ago.

'In July 1856, a boat with two crew, taking three families to start new lives in London, left Polruan. Seven adults and ten children in all. The day had started sunny and fair, much like this one, but with a stiff westerly wind blowing. Before the party departed, dark clouds were gathering on the far horizon and a noticeable sea-swell had developed. Barometers were dropping and locals knew a dramatic change in the weather was on the way, but the hope was it would just be a passing squall. The party set off in a lugger owned by my ancestor, Cornelius Penhale, called the *Rosebud*. She was a fine vessel, clinker built and forty feet in length…'

Charlie didn't hear the rest of the description. As soon as he heard the name *Rosebud*, his mind began working overtime. Where had he heard it before? He tried to think of all the boats he'd seen on his trips across the river, and the fishing trawlers under repair in the boatyard next to the quay. It wouldn't come to him, but he knew it was somehow significant...

'So when the storm did hit the coast, it came fast and hard, catching everyone by surprise. The *Rosebud* was caught close to a lee shore...'

'What's that?' Charlie asked.

'It's what you call the coast when the wind is blowing towards it, isn't it, Mr Penhale?' Sue offered.

'Quite right. Sailing boats obviously find it much harder to sail into the wind rather than when it's behind them. If it's trying to blow you towards the shore – what they call a "lee shore" – you need plenty of room to manoeuvre or you're in big trouble. Hence the term needing "leeway". So, caught out, the skipper of the *Rosebud* didn't have sufficient leeway to work his way clear. A skipper can only tack – steering left and right and try to make a bit of progress with each turn; but that takes room and time – and the *Rosebud* didn't have enough of either.'

The Creep was starting to talk like someone presenting a TV documentary now. He stood up at the side of the water taxi, pointing theatrically to the rugged shoreline.

'Not enough time or room...' he declared, pausing for effect, 'to avoid being dashed onto *BLACKBOTTLE ROCK*!'

The dramatic effect was somewhat spoiled when the wind blew the long hairs Penhale had carefully arranged over his bald head all over the place and it looked as if he'd had an electric shock. Charlie glanced at the water taxi man, and thought he seemed to be hiding a smirk; Charlie guessed he'd heard and seen all this performance many times before. But while the Creep was desperately trying to flatten his hair back in place as he droned on about the history of wrecks in the area, Charlie did turn his attention to the ominous rock formation jutting out into the sea. It wasn't hard to imagine a powerful wind and waves throwing them towards it. A small craft like theirs would be little more than matchwood in seconds.

'Cornelius Penhale had noticed the weather turning, and, fearing for the safety of the men, women and children on board the *Rosebud*, ignored the risk to his own life and decided to put to sea in a little boat on his own to see what he could do.'

'That must have taken incredible courage,' Sue commented.

'My ancestor was a courageous man, in business and in life,' Penhale said, puffing out his chest a little. 'I'd like to think those qualities have been passed down through the generations!'

Charlie had to grit his teeth to stop himself letting out a derisive snort as he listened to the little man with his upturned nose and glasses that looked like he'd found them in a joke shop ramble on. He couldn't imagine the Creep saving anyone but himself in a crisis.

'Battling through the storm, Cornelius guided his little vessel through the crashing waves until he arrived more or less where we are now and saw the terrible plight of the *Rosebud*. By the time he had arrived, she had already hit the rocks and been holed, but was still afloat. Some had already been thrown overboard and were lost from sight. With great skill and bravery, he took his boat as close in as he could and managed drag a man called Isaac Trewin on board. Isaac himself was clutching his young son William. As he was doing this, a tremendous wave swept the *Rosebud* against Blackbottle Rock once more. She was smashed to pieces, and those left on board were not seen again until their bodies were washed ashore several miles down the coast some days later.'

The stationary taxi bobbed in the water as they all solemnly surveyed the scene of the terrible event. Even in calm conditions, the skipper had to keep blipping the engine every now and then to stop the boat washing towards the rocky shore. Charlie could easily imagine mums and dads fighting to stay afloat with the churning sea crashing over their heads – at the same time desperately floundering to reach for little children being tossed around like limp pieces of seaweed…

Henry Penhale made a few concluding remarks while Sue scribbled busily in her notebook, then it was time for them to turn the head of the boat back towards the Fowey River. As they departed, Charlie thought he heard something…

Anguished cries, faintly, distantly mingling with the rising note of the engine and the washing of the waves over Blackbottle Rock.

At first he thought it must be seagulls, but then a deep man's voice cut through the general murmur. Whatever he was shouting was still faint and carried away on the wind, but the wrathful, accusing tone was unmistakable. Charlie twisted sharply, looking back, but all he saw was a miniature rainbow created by white sea-spray cascading over the rock.

'Did you hear that?'

Sue looked up from her notebook. 'Hear what?

Charlie turned to Penhale, who seemed distinctly unnerved and avoided his gaze. 'No. I heard nothing.'

'But—'

'Dave,' he called to the skipper of the water taxi, 'I've got a group to take round Saint Finbarus church in half an hour.'

Dave duly increased the speed of the boat, and Charlie watched Blackbottle Rock getting smaller until they turned into the estuary and it vanished from view.

eight

Rosebud…

The boat that was wrecked on Blackbottle Rock and this old house bore the same name.

Charlie let his gaze wander up from the wooden door with its peeling blue paint, past the upper floor to the dormer window of the attic. It looked blank and lifeless now. He'd wondered how such a run-down place could be a holiday cottage, as advertised on the little faded sign in the front window. Ever eager to oblige, Sue had looked into it, and discovered from the company they'd booked their own place with, that it used to be managed by them but was removed from their lists because they had trouble getting people to stay there. They hadn't seemed keen to explain why, and it simply appeared that the owner – a Londoner who rarely visited the village – hadn't bothered to take the sign out.

Charlie could guess why no one would stay there. What he'd love to know was how Henry Penhale was connected with it. How had he got a key to get in? Why had he been prowling about inside? How did it fit in with the face at the window, the page he tore from the burial register, the rug he'd taken into his storeroom?

*

'He was telling me he's going to unveil a plaque here on Friday,' Sue was saying. She, Dad and Charlie were sitting on a bench, licking at dribbling ice creams, watching the boats on the river. He hadn't been paying much attention to what she was saying, but now his ears pricked up. Trouble was, he didn't want to let on that he was interested in anything she had to say…

'I'm sure he'll make certain there's a photographer or two to record the historic event,' Dad commented with a wry smile.

'Don't be such a wet blanket,' Sue chided. 'But you're right – he's a bit full of himself. Creepy, even...'

Creepy? Now Charlie *had* to drop his uninterested act. 'Who? Who's creepy?'

'Oh, I shouldn't have said it like that. I'm sure he's a very nice man when you get to know him...'

'You're talking about Henry Penhale, aren't you?'

'Yes, but Charlie—'

'Don't backtrack now,' Dad teased. 'When Chas was upstairs you were saying you thought he was a smarmy so-and-so in the boat this morning!'

'Told you,' Charlie muttered.

'He paid for the hire of the boat, and he gave me lots of useful information for my book...'

'All we've got to do now is find out who he murdered and we'll get him put away for good!'

'Dad!' said Charlie. He could be a pain in the backside when he wanted to be.

'Anyway, Charlie,' Sue said, checking her watch. 'I've got a mission for you this afternoon – should you choose to accept it.'

'Oh?' He was quickly trying to plan ahead, think of excuses why he couldn't do it – whatever it was.

'Your dad and I are going across to Fowey – I've got some delving to do in the library. That'll be pretty boring for you, but I was thinking we could meet up there if you go by a different route and do a job for me at Lanteglos church.'

Lanteglos Church – the place the burial register was stolen from. Where he was sure the *Creep* had stolen the burial register.

'I might. What sort of job?'

'Take some pictures. You're a pretty good photographer and I'll need some photos for the book. You can take my camera.' She lifted the strap of the expensive digital SLR from around her neck and held it out to him.

At that moment he heard the 'new message' tone on his

phone. 'What do you mean by "a different route"?'

'You know the car ferry we used when we arrived? There's a walk through the woods – very popular with hikers – that takes you right to it, and Lanteglos church is just a slight detour along the way.'

Charlie was glancing at his phone while Sue explained this. The text was from Wei-Li:

We've got news! Can u come?

Charlie took the camera from her. 'Okay, I'll do it.'

*

The Hall Walk, as it was called, was longer than he'd imagined. It started near the back of the noisy boatyard and led up into the woods that covered the hill overlooking the river. He was following it with a little map Sue had given him – one they'd bought from Henry Penhale's own Beachcomber gift shop – but the path was pretty easy to follow anyway. It was surprising how quickly they left behind the bustle of tourists and clangs and bangs of the boatyard. Despite the fact that this was a popular walk there was no one else about today, and Charlie began to feel as if he were in a much more ancient, undisturbed place. In places the tall trees and tangled undergrowth kept out much of the sunlight, and deadened the sounds of the river and the two communities of Polruan and Fowey on either side of it. There were some steep climbs, but then everything around here seemed to involve steep walks so Charlie was getting used to that. Eventually, he came to a wooden signpost that pointed to a place called Pont in one direction and Lanteglos church the other. Consulting his map, he saw that after visiting the church he would have to come back this way to get to the Bodinnick Ferry by way of Pont.

Pont... All the names around here seemed to be so different that it was like being abroad. At first, it annoyed him. Now, it was beginning to grow on him…

A few minutes more walking brought him his first view of the church, nestling in the trees. It was clearly ancient, built from a pale grey stone. In the grassy cemetery surrounding it stood moss-covered gravestones and crosses, many of them leaning precariously, like drunken old men in mouldy overcoats. For the first time since Charlie had arrived in Cornwall, a grey cloud drifted across the sun. The church and grave markers cast eerie shadows, and unless it brightened, the outdoors pictures weren't going to come out nearly as well as he'd expected. But he dutifully walked around the churchyard, taking snaps from different angles. For a moment, the sun broke through and Charlie hurried back to re-take some pictures. He managed to get several decent ones, then more clouds moved in and the gloom settled on the church once again. It was only now that he spotted something he had missed the first time: a large gravestone and a word that jumped out at him as soon as his eyes fell upon it.

Rosebud

Charlie switched the camera off to save the battery and knelt down so he could read the inscription on the weathered slab:

Sacred to the memory of
EDWARD EDGECOMBE born 1819
& his wife SARAH EDGECOMBE born 1819
of this parish
& their children
EDWARD born 1846
JOHN born 1847
EMMA born 1850
THOMAS born 1852
Tragically perished in the sinking of the lugger ROSEBUD and buried 25 April 1856
"For there is nothing covered that shall not be revealed; and hid that shall not be known" Matthew 10:26

Charlie gazed pensively at the old monument, imagining the people gathered round this grave in 1856. The youngest of the drowned children would have been no more than four when the *Rosebud* went down, and even the oldest was younger than Charlie. He still felt sorry for himself at losing his mother seven years ago, but the cold sea has swallowed up this whole family. None of them lived to feel sorry for themselves, nor tell the tale.

But *did* the gravestone tell some sort of tale?

What a weird thing to put on a gravestone: *Nothing covered that shall not be revealed, hid that shall not be known…*

What was covered or hidden?

Charlie crouched down to take a couple of photographs of the headstone. On the second click of the shutter, he thought he heard someone coming from the church and quickly twisted round. There was no one there – but he felt sure the main door to the church had been shut when he first arrived. Now it was a few inches ajar.

He rose and listened, all his senses telling him that someone had passed behind him. But all he could hear was the chirping of the birds and the first splatters of rain hitting the gravestones around him. Suddenly, he wasn't so keen to get pictures of the inside of church. But he'd promised Sue. He took a deep breath, then strode down the path between more graves to the arched doorway. The door itself was an old, heavy wooden one and creaked like something out of a horror film when he pushed it open. The colder air was noticeable as soon as he took the first few tentative steps inside. Two rows of pews ran down the centre of the building towards an altar covered with a white and gold cloth, behind and above which was a large stained-glass window. A row of stone arches divided the main body of the church from aisles on either side, and Charlie wandered along the aisle closest to him, almost as if he felt he had no right to encroach into the nave itself. The rain was getting heavier now, rattling against the roof and windows as he shuffled forwards, halting occasionally to take more pictures. He was still on edge, and it occurred to him that the sound of the rain would drown out the footsteps of anyone coming up behind him…

Ahead on the right he saw a door with a little plaque on it, and when he got closer he saw it said *Vestry*. Charlie didn't know what a vestry was, but he had an overwhelming urge to find out. Again, this door was ajar and at first he just gently pressed it enough to peer inside, in case someone was working in there. At that moment, he heard a car engine roar into life in the lane outside. It made him twitch and he inadvertently pushed the door harder than he'd intended. It swung wide open and, as it did so, the doorknob fell without warning, clattering and bouncing to the stone floor with an echo that resounded throughout the church. He hadn't even touched it. Charlie gasped, and the rush of adrenaline was so sudden and powerful he felt for a second as if he might faint.

As the growl of the fleeing car's engine died away, he saw why the doorknob had fallen off. There were deep gouge marks and splintered wood, both around the hole where the knob had been, and on the adjacent doorframe. Someone had broken in. He knew it had happened before, when the burial register was stolen – but these marks were fresh. What could have been taken this time? Surely the Creep wouldn't risk it again? He knew people stole stuff like gold candlesticks from churches, and he tried to tell himself it must have been an 'ordinary' burglary.

He could hear his heartbeat throbbing in his eardrums, but now he knew there was no one in the vestry he risked looking inside. It was just like a little office, with shelves of books, a desk and filing cabinet. But it was what was on the desk that caught Charlie's eye. It was a large, thick old leather-bound book. But not just any book. He'd only seen it once before, but he knew what it was. Someone has returned the church's stolen burial register.

While he was still trying to take this in, he heard voices.

A man and woman on the path outside the church, getting closer.

For a second, Charlie froze to the spot. If he ran, he'd look guilty. He wanted to do the honest thing – stay, explain. But he'd still look guilty. They'd never believe it wasn't him that had broken into the vestry. People never believed kids. They'd probably think he was the one who stole the book in the first place. He ran.

The instant he left the vestry, he heard the squeaking of the front door and the voices echoing as they entered the church. Too late. All he could do was dive behind the pews. The polished floor squeaked loudly as he skidded along – but the couple were too busy talking to notice.

'…so she asked me if I'd organise the summer fair and *the quiz night this year,'* the woman grumbled. *'I'm mean, It's not as if she's the only one who has a full-time job. In fact I work more hours than she does.'*

'You don't want to go saying that to her, my dear. You know what she's like!'

They were walking down the centre of the church, coming almost level with him. The pews provided some cover, but some part of his body *had* to be visible. All he could do was keep flat and dead still – but if one of them were even to glance his way…

'Well I won't do the cake sale, I really won't. I was talking to Alice about it on Sunday and she said the same thing. She said – hang on… What's that?'

Charlie tensed so much his stomach muscles hurt. He couldn't bear to look up.

Stay or run? That's all that was going through his mind.

'There, look…'

Decide!

He began to raise himself up. They sounded elderly. They'd never catch him, and if he sprinted without looking back they might not even get a look at his face.

'The vestry door…'

'Oh, my Lord. Not again!'

They had gone past – they hadn't seen him!

He tiptoed down the aisle as quickly as he could, listening to them examining the door, picking the doorknob up, chuntering in dismay. He even felt somehow guilty, as if he really had been the one responsible. Part of him wanted to go back, explain, tell them who he thought had done it.

But as soon as he got to the door of the church, he ran out into the rain as fast as he could.

nine

There were still lots of dark clouds around, but the sun was pouring through gaps and making the damp pavements steam by the time Charlie reached Treffry House. The walk from the church had led him down the hill through the trees to Pont Pil, which turned out to be a little stream with a low footbridge running over it beside a big, secluded house. The path then went back up the hill towards Bodinnick and the ferry, with terrific views at the top across the river towards Polruan and Fowey. Charlie took more shots from up there.

As on his last visit, the gates to Treffry House were open. And also as before, there was someone in the courtyard – but this time it wasn't the man he'd learned was Wei-Li's wealthy businessman father, nor the woman whom he hired to come in to clean and cook. It was Wei-Li herself, and the sight brought Charlie to a halt.

She was in the centre of the yard, wearing what looked like a sort of kung-fu uniform: it was deep blue with what looked like dragons in gold, in a silky material that shimmered in the sunlight as she moved. But it was the *way* she was moving. It seemed to be some sort of set of martial arts moves, but in slow motion: gentle and graceful, yet somehow powerful. Sometimes she would raise a foot as if performing a slow karate kick, then spin round with the foot still in the air: controlled, perfectly balanced. She snaked around an imaginary circle, creeping down, rising up, turning, and all the time the movements of her arms and legs were synchronised perfectly. The different martial arts postures flowed seamlessly from one to another – but then, while Wei-Li still had her back to Charlie, she stopped as if someone had pressed a 'pause' button.

'You can come in you know, Charlie.'

He couldn't see her face, but he knew she was grinning as she spoke. 'I didn't want to disturb you. It looks gr—' He checked himself. Didn't want to sound too soppy. 'It must be hard to learn.'

She resumed her movements. 'A few months to learn, but a lifetime to perfect. I'll teach you if you like.'

'Huh – not sure I can afford a lifetime of lessons…'

She smiled as she resumed for another minute before finally coming to a halt. She brought her feet together, rested her hands on her lower abdomen, one on top of the other, then bowed in Charlie's general direction.

'It's something my grandfather always said. *Months to learn, a lifetime to perfect.* My dad learned from him too but he was always too busy with his business to keep it up, so Grandfather Lu taught me. What he meant was you need to search for the inner meaning. You're always learning.'

'Is it some kind of kung fu?'

'In a way. Tai Chi – you must have heard of it.'

'I think so.'

'Want a drink? Juice or something?'

Only now did Charlie realise how thirsty he had become since setting off from Polruan at least a couple of hours ago. 'Yes please – orange if you've got it.'

A few minutes later they were sitting on a park bench-type seat against the wall of the house, bathed in sunshine. As she always seemed to, Wei-Li had assumed a cross-legged posture.

'Where's Mohan?'

'Oh, he got bored and went home.'

'Ah, sorry. It took longer than it should have because I had a job to do on the way.'

'Don't worry. Mohan's got a restless mind. Easily bored. What job was it?'

'Well, when you hear what I saw you won't mind how long it took me to get here.'

He began by telling her about the Edgecombe family grave,

and the feeling that someone had left the church and crept past him while he was looking at it.

'It was the Creep. I *know* it was. And there's more...'

'The Creep?'

'Oh, er... That's the nickname I gave Henry Penhale,' he replied, rather sheepishly.

Wei-Li laughed, and it was like the most beautiful song imaginable.

'And?'

'What? Ah, yes...' He couldn't remember the exact wording on the gravestone, so he turned the camera on to check the picture. '*For there is nothing covered that shall not be revealed; and hid that shall not be known. Matthew 10:26*. It's from the Bible.'

'Really? I thought it was from *Harry Potter*...'

Charlie gave her a quizzical look – until he saw the twinkle in her dark eyes and realised she was teasing him. 'What's been "covered" – that's what I want to know.'

'After all these years it might not be possible to find out. Maybe the family had a dark secret.'

'Well, maybe the Creep thinks it *can* be found out – otherwise he wouldn't sneaking around doing all this stuff. And just after I heard him, or whoever it was, leaving the church, I found there'd been another break-in. Only this time, something's been *put back*, not stolen.'

'The burial register.'

'Yep. Doesn't make sense to me, but he's returned it.'

'Maybe it's his conscience. However creepy he is, he doesn't sound like your average robber. A historical thing like that can never be replaced, so perhaps he got what he needed and wanted it to be put back where it belonged.'

Charlie shrugged. 'We're no closer to finding out.'

'Maybe we are. A bit, anyway. Mohan has discovered that the Penhale family once owned Rosebud Cottage.'

'That fits I suppose, seeing as old Cornelius owned a boat with the same name.'

'Henry could still own the cottage, for all we know.'

'No. Sue told me the family sold it. Someone in London owns it now.'

'Sue?'

He realised he'd never mentioned her. He rarely did. 'She's my – she's Dad's girlfriend. For now, anyway.'

Wei-Li lowered her eyes. 'I'm sorry I upset you when I said that thing about your mum and the angel. I pick up these things, and it's hard to know whether it's best to tell people or not…'

'I'm kind of glad you did tell me.'

'Can I tell you something else?'

Charlie felt his heart take a leap. 'I suppose…'

'If you give Sue a chance, it may well all work out.'

'You don't understand. It's like she's put a spell on Dad with her smiles and her nice ways. He'll see through it eventually.'

'Oh, I didn't realise it was as bad as that. Smiles and nice ways? Before you know it, it will be presents and laughter and there'll be no stopping her evil ways.'

Charlie nudged her playfully – but a little too hard. She was about to topple off the edge of the bench, and he caught her arm. Then he wondered why she was still looking at him in some sort of meaningful way – until he realised he was still holding her slender limb. He quickly let it go.

'Sorry…' He felt himself reddening.

'Don't be.' She sprang up from her cross-legged position as lithely as a cat. 'We need to let Mohan know the latest.'

Wei-Li slipped indoors, and re-emerged tapping the screen of her mobile. Within seconds she was recounting Charlie's story to her FPI partner, and she put the call on speakerphone so that Charlie could hear.

'I'm not sure what we should do next, apart from keeping a close eye on Henry Penhale.'

Mohan's breath rasped out of the speaker like static as he

thought for a moment. 'There's one important thing we're overlooking…'

'What's that?' asked Wei-Li

'Charlie's obsession with Penhale has made us forget our original interest in what was happening in Polruan and what we usually do.'

'Excuse Mohan's rudeness,' Wei-Li said to Charlie with a wink.

'I'm not rude – I just don't waste words like most people. We are a paranormal investigation team. There's something paranormal going in the area around Rosebud Cottage *and* it might involve Penhale. The ghost sightings are probably related to the disaster – I'm surprised we never thought of that. We should approach it the way we would normally – carry out a *ghost hunt*.'

'We said we'd help Charlie, and there's no proof that the hauntings *are* connected to Henry Penhale himself.'

'Er, actually…' began Charlie awkwardly. He told them about the face at the attic window and Penhale's terror, and the voices off Blackbottle Rock.

'Why didn't you tell us?' Mohan's tinny, irate voice trumpeted out of the phone.

'Because I thought it would sound silly – I'm still not sure either any of it was really to do with ghosts, or just my imagination.'

'I think Mohan's right,' Wei-Li decided after giving it some thought. 'Charlie, you aren't the first to see that face at the window. It's one of the reports we were looking into when you arrived in Polruan. We need to get our equipment together and carry out a nighttime vigil as soon as possible. Will you join us?'

Charlie felt a chill pass through his body. A real *ghost hunt*?

He tried to sound as cool as possible. 'Course I will…'

ten

Charlie felt the gentle warmth of the sun caressing his face, and luxuriated in the butterscotch glow playing on the lids of his closed eyes. He turned over and tried to go back to sleep, but by now he had also become conscious of the soothing but insistent rush of water on the little beach nearby, washing up and slipping back, again and again to its own timeless rhythm. It drew him into wakefulness.

A perfect summer's morning – for a few glorious seconds. Why did that lurking feeling of dread in pit of his stomach always spoil things these days? Like storm clouds creeping across a pristine blue sky, darker thoughts crowded into his mind, and he remembered.

He had no mother any more. He was half an orphan. His dad was living with a witch. He was spending a holiday in a dead-end town. Okay, it had become more interesting of late – but scary spooks and robberies weren't exactly what he had been looking for on this holiday. Oh, and tonight he was supposed to be actually going in search of ghosts who made hateful faces at windows.

Breakfast was an uneasy time. He had butterflies in his stomach about tonight, imagining Rosebud's evil spirits possessing him, the way people in films were. And he had to fib to Dad and Sue about why he didn't want to go with them on a trip to the beach at a place called Par. Dad wanted to go body-boarding and have a picnic – but Wei-Li and Mohan were coming over to plan how they were going to get in to the old cottage...

'I'm feeling whacked. I didn't sleep very well last night for some reason, and then the seagulls woke me up as soon as it was light. Anyway, Wei-Li and Mohan are coming across on the ferry later and I said I'd meet up with them...'

'Seagulls? I didn't hear them,' Dad said.

'Your snoring probably drowned it out,' said Sue.

'I don't snore!'

'*You do!*' Charlie and Sue said virtually together. Charlie found himself grinning conspiratorially with her. He was kind of annoyed with himself. It was like giving in to her. But it felt strangely nice, too.

'Charlie can go and see his new friends. We can do Par tomorrow if the weather holds. We could have a stroll around – and there's still a few things I want to find out for my book anyway about the Blackbottle Rock disaster anyway.'

'The weather isn't going to hold according to the forecast,' Dad said. 'But I suppose there'll be another chance before we leave.'

Charlie could tell Dad was trying hard to hide how disappointed he was at not doing a family thing together, and he suddenly felt guilty and dishonest. But then, if Dad only knew how important this was he would understand.

'There's something odd about it, you know,' said Sue half to herself, chewing on a piece of toast.

'Odd about what?' Dad asked.

'This Blackbottle Rock business.'

Charlie tried to hide his sudden extra interest.

'See, most of the locals are proud of Cornelius Penhale and love talking about how he single-handedly saved who he could from the storm. But one or two older folk seem reluctant to talk about it – especially about Cornelius himself. Whenever I try to press them they clam up.'

'I suppose they're sick of hearing about him,' said Dad. 'Henry Penhale's made such a fuss about the story that newcomers would think there's nothing else to the history of Polruan. It'd get on my nerves eventually.'

'You could be right, but I wonder... One old boy I was chatting to in the mini-market muttered something under his breath as he walked away that sounded like *"It wasn't the storm that killed 'em…"* or words to that effect.'

'Well, you said yourself you didn't hear him properly. Surely he was saying, "It *was* the storm that killed them",' Dad said. 'Meaning "*What more is there to say?*".'

Sue seemed to accept that she must have misheard the old man's words.

Charlie wasn't so sure.

*

Charlie leaned against the rails lining the quay, watching for the approach of the Polruan ferry. There were plenty of people about and the Creep had to be busy in his shop, so Charlie wasn't too worried about any awkward encounters – though he made sure to stand at an angle where he had the Beachcomber in his peripheral vision. If the weather was going to change, there was no sign of it yet. The clouds of yesterday lurked on the horizon, but the sun was floating above the green hills where he'd followed the Hall Walk, reflecting so dazzlingly on the water that he couldn't look at the river without screwing up his eyes. The sound of hammering and clanging echoed around the boatyard on the other side of the quay, where a big, rusty old fishing boat was being repaired. Down on the 'beach' – which was probably no more than half the size of a football pitch that disappeared altogether at high tide – a bronzed young man and woman hauled sleek canoes out into the water and clambered aboard, paddling effortlessly away in the direction of the Pont Pill creek he'd crossed yesterday.

A large pleasure boat motored majestically in from the sea, and once it had passed Charlie saw the orange and white ferry making its approach. His phone bleeped before it docked. It was a text from Mohan – but since they would soon be talking face-to-face, Charlie didn't bother to read it and but the phone back in the pocket of his shorts.

He walked to the top of the stone steps as the ferry disgorged its passengers – only to find that neither Mohan nor Wei-Li were there. What he did notice, though, was a rather scruffy youth of about fourteen or fifteen. He wore a sort of wannabe gangster uniform of baggy jeans hanging halfway down his backside, and an over-sized baseball cap on sideways, partially covering a severe haircut that looked as if he'd done it himself. Charlie avoided making eye contact, but sensed that the youth was sizing him up as he climbed the step steps. Charlie fixed his eyes on Treffry House in the distance, willing his friends to arrive by some other means pretty soon. But all the time the dodgy kid was lurking nearby and, Charlie knew, sizing him up. He was the sort who would wait until you finally looked his way, then growl, 'You lookin' at me?' He wasn't going to give him the excuse.

He slipped away from the rails as a group of four middle-aged women hikers passed him, and followed them past the Beachcomber and the Schooner pub to the tiny 'square' near the bottom of Fore Street, the road leading up the hill out of Polruan. The plan was to hang around on the bench opposite Crumpets teashop – but the youth had followed him, and was heading his way. Charlie made to move off again.

'Hey,' his stalker called curtly.

He could have pretended not to hear, but he knew he'd only be putting off the inevitable. He turned to face the youth.

'Charlie?'

'How did you know my name?'

'Didn't 'ee get the text? They said they'd let 'ee know.' He had a real old-fashioned Cornish accent. Like a pirate.

Charlie whipped his phone out.

Will be bit late. Talk to Kev

Typical Mohan – short and to the point.

'You're Kev?' Charlie asked, and received a brisk nod in reply. 'Are you in the FPI as well?'

Kev sniggered. 'All that ghost crap? I sometimes help 'em out.'

'What for, if you don't believe in ghosts?'

'Money.'

There wasn't really any answer to that.

'So what help do they need today?'

Kev ignored his question. 'Do 'ee believe in 'em?'

It sounded almost like a challenge, and Charlie decided to hedge his bets until he got to know Kev a bit better.

'Not sure. Never seen one.'

'We're gonna see about gettin' into this cottage. That's what I'm for.'

'Do you know the owner, then? Can you get hold of the key?'

'Yeah, the key.' Kev smiled darkly. 'Summen' like that.'

'Believe in UFOs?' Kev demanded.

'Nah,' Charlie replied, still playing it safe. Or so he thought.

'Well they *DO exist,* see?' said Kev, raising his voice. Cos I seen one, right?'

'Oh, right…'

'It were over Penzance. Two lights, it had: green and red, blinkin' on and off.'

Even Charlie knew that *all* planes displayed green and red lights. 'Oh…'

'And it weren't no plane,' Kev added as if aware of the weakness to his story. 'Cos it were *completely silent.*'

'How big were lights?'

'Tiny.

'Hmm.'

'But I saw 'em, all right. Extratorrential, that's what it was. Show me where this place is.'

Charlie led Kev up West Street, passing by the little lane where his own holiday cottage lay, until they came to Rosebud. Charlie held back across the street, but Kev walked boldly up to the house. First, he peered in through the window, then he scrutinised the front door closely before re-joining Charlie.

'It's cool,' he reported.

'Great,' Charlie replied – though he wasn't quite sure what was cool. Perhaps he just needed reassuring that it really was the cottage for which he could get the key. His phone began to ring.

'Sorry we're late, Charlie.' It was Wei-Li. 'I had to run an errand for Dad. Where are you?'

'Outside Rosebud Cottage – with Kev.'

'Be with you soon.'

It only took them a minute to come.

'We shouldn't stay here too long,' said Mohan. 'Don't want to draw attention to ourselves.'

'Kev says he can get hold of the key for it,' Charlie explained.

Kev made a sort of half-snorting, half-guffawing noise, and Wei-Li and Mohan exchanged glances.

'Key?' Wei-Li queried.

'I thought that was the idea…'

'We've already attempted to gain permission to enter the property through official channels,' Mohan explained, shoving his glasses up his nose. He waited while a young couple with a pushchair passed by before continuing. 'And we were denied by people who assume young people can't act in a responsible manner and aren't capable of ridding a village of a supernatural problem.'

Charlie's spirits sank. All this fuss, and the ghost watch was over before it started.

'So Kev's going to gain entrance for us using his own methods.'

'*Gain entrance…*' Charlie gawped. 'You mean – BREAK IN!'

'*Ssshh,*' Charlie' said Wei-Li looking up and down the street. 'Let's go down to the quay.'

Once they were sitting on a seat overlooking the river, away from anyone else, Wei-Li explained the situation to him.

'It's not something we enjoy doing, but we believe that ghosts are souls trapped in limbo, unable to move on for some reason, and we feel we have to do anything in our power to release them.

The house is empty, and we aren't going to steal or damage anything...'

'*She* thinks ghosts are trapped souls that need to go to the light,' Mohan corrected. 'I subscribe to the Stone Tape theory myself.'

'Stone tape?' Charlie asked. He noticed Kev had grown bored with the conversation already and was somehow managing to play a game on his mobile and pick his nose at the same time.

'It's the idea,' said Wei-Li, 'that ghosts aren't spirits of the dead, but more like a recording of the people's energies and emotions – especially powerful ones such as a murder or tragic death. The energies are somehow soaked up by the surroundings – stone, brick, wood – and are triggered into replaying every so often. That's his theory – it's just that I know mine's right.'

It was the closest Charlie had seen Wei-Li come to anger. She obviously cared deeply about this subject.

'*How* do you know?'

'Because I've been in contact with spirits. In ancient China, everyone believed in honouring the spirits of the ancestors. Certain gifted people could communicate with them, a gift that ran in families – my grandfather was one, and he helped me to develop the skill. I'm not very good – it's like a very bad telephone line where you can't quite make everything out. But I know it's true.'

'Whereas *my* theory is based on *proper science,*' Mohan declared flatly.

Charlie didn't know who to believe – just that he had a strange urge to punch Mohan on the nose...

'Look, kids,' grumbled Kev, still playing his game. 'Are we on for tonight or not?'

Wei-Li looked to Charlie for his answer.

Deliberately seeking out ghosts was bad enough, but getting into a house without permission. It was madness, it was ridiculous. And if Wei-Li hadn't been involved...

'All right – but the first sign of trouble and I'm off.'

'Thanks, Charlie.'

She gave him a quick hug, and he could feel the imprint of her soft, dainty little hands on his shoulders after she took them away.

'Oh…' he said as an afterthought.

'What now?' Kev demanded impatiently.

'We should start with the attic…'

eleven

Charlie spent a couple of hours on his own in the cottage, waiting for Dad and Sue to return. He googled ghosts, spirits, the 'Stone Tape' theory, but there was just so much stuff out there, so many sites, so many different explanations about what ghosts were or if they even existed, that he began to suffer from information overload and went back to looking at the boats on the river.

But the Creep's storeroom was in his line of sight down below, and he couldn't stop thinking about what connection he had with the ghosts Wei-Li and Mohan believed haunted Rosebud Cottage, Penhale's old family home. Where did the stolen burial register come into it? Burial registers were for dead people, and ghosts were dead people. Or not. The rug didn't seem to fit in, though. Was that just a random event? Anyone can take carry an old rug about. But he'd seemed so secretive about it. The storeroom didn't need a rug – probably wasn't big enough for that one – and it wasn't as if he was taking it to a tip or some place to get rid of it.

He wandered back outside – through the alleyway and out to the harbour. It was bright, but the dark clouds that had never quite gone away were gathering out to sea and seemed to be slowly creeping inland. Then Charlie spotted Dad and Sue down on the beach. He had never really seen them acting naturally together without him; spying on them was kind of a thrill at first, but soon started to feel not quite right. They were holding hands like teenage lovers, casually chatting and looking as happy and relaxed as he had ever seen them. Okay, it was soppy – but then again, they looked kind of *right* together, and that was painful to admit. The unwanted thought pushed its way into his head that he had been so obsessed with himself that he hadn't really been thinking of *Dad's* happiness. It made him feel selfish in an ugly kind of way, which he was sure he wasn't, but... Charlie snapped out of it, turning away from them.

It wasn't long, though, before they appeared on quayside and spotted him. Dad went into the Lugger to get some drinks, leaving him sitting uncomfortably alone with Sue on a little wall overlooking the beach.

'What do you make of him, then?' she asked.

'Dad?' Charlie countered, a little alarmed.

'No, chump – Henry Penhale!'

'He's weird. Don't like him.'

'Neither do I. And he's hiding something.'

Charlie sat up. 'What?'

'He loves boasting about Cornelius, basking in the limelight of being the descendant of a local hero – yet there are places he doesn't want to go when you try to talk to him about it.'

'*Now* do you believe I saw him rip a page out of the burial register?'

'I always did.'

'Oh... Thanks.'

'I believed you, but it just didn't make sense for someone who is Mr Local History to go defacing old historical records. I even thought there must be some sort of innocent explanation – maybe he was getting rid of a damaged page with nothing of importance on it or something. But now I have my doubts.'

Dad arrived with beers for the adults and a juice for Charlie. 'Doubts about what?'

'Henry Penhale.'

'I was just looking at a picture of the bloke Cornelius Penhale saved. Old black and white one on the wall of the pub.'

'Am I allowed to go inside and look?' Charlie asked.

'Sure.' Dad slid off the wall and handed his beer to Sue. 'Come on – I'll show you.'

There were just a couple of locals sitting at the bar inside the rather dimly lit, olde worlde pub, with its wooden beams and a real fireplace at one end. Old photographs lined the walls – mostly ships and boats on the Fowey River, but a few bearing the faces of local characters. Dad led Charlie to the left of the bar, where above a seat there hung a picture, blotched and faded with age. It featured a rather thin man with a bushy moustache. Although he wore that rather stern expression look that all people in Victorian pictures seemed to have, there was the faintest of smiles on his lips and Charlie suspected he was actually a kindly man. Beside him stood a boy wearing a thick, uncomfortable looking jacket. It seemed as if his hair had been especially plastered into a state of artificial neatness for the picture, and he looked half-bewildered, half-startled to have a camera pointed at him. There was a short, printed caption underneath that had been added in more recent times, though still many years ago:

> *Isaac Trewin & his son William the day before departing Polruan on the* Rosebud *for London in 1856. Mr Trewin was left penniless when a fire destroyed his chandlery shop, then suffered further hardship when the* Rosebud *foundered on Black Bottle Rock in a storm. Thanks to the heroic efforts of Mr Cornelius Penhale, father and son were saved and able to start their new life in the capital after all.*

'That's funny…' Sue said with a frown.

'What is?' asked Charlie.

'It says Isaac Trewin was "left penniless" – but when I was doing my research I kept coming across his name, and I assumed he was well off like Cornelius. He certainly ended up with a thriving chandler's shop in London – he even opened a second branch. He started a charitable fund to help the widows of the Polruan and Fowey men lost at sea, and he paid for the gravestones of every single person who drowned in the Blackbottle Rock disaster.'

'I've seen some of them when I was taking pictures for you at Lanteglos church!' Charlie told her.

'He must have used the money from his new business to pay for everything,' Dad suggested, but Sue shook her head.

'He hadn't even set off for London again when he paid for the headstones and started the charity – yet he was supposed to have lost everything even *before* the boat sank.'

Charlie searched the faces of Isaac Trewin and his son.

I'm glad you survived and did well – but where did you get the money from? What really happened at Blackbottle Rock?

*

A sleepover. That was how Charlie managed to wangle it. And it wasn't even a lie – just not the whole truth. He *was* going to stay the night with Mohan and Wei-Li at her house, it was just that there was the small matter of a ghost watch at Rosebud Cottage on the way. He didn't feel proud of himself for deceiving them, but Charlie felt this was something that had to be done and it was the only way. If anything went wrong he was literally seconds away from Dad and Sue.

They met at the appointed time on the quay. It was dark, but not that late and people were still using the ferry to go over to Fowey where there were more pubs and eating-places. Thankfully, the rest of Polruan was quiet, as it usually was in the evening, though as they made their way to East Street Charlie noticed a light on in the flat above the Beachcomber. There were a couple of smokers sitting cradling their pints and chatting outside Polruan's other pub, the Martin's Arms, but there was a kink in the claustrophobically narrow street which hid Rosebud Cottage from their view.

As soon as they were outside the place, Ken rummaged in his pockets. 'Turn round,' he ordered them.

'What?' said Charlie, annoyed at being told what to do by this chav.

'It's better that we don't see what he does,' Wei-Li whispered.

He felt like a lemon, but they all dutifully faced the opposite side of the street and waited. Charlie heard some clicking and scraping, and a couple of grunts of effort and concentration from Kev – then the turning of a handle. They all wheeled round, and the door of Rosebud Cottage was gaping open to reveal a black, uninviting void.

'That's me done,' muttered Kev, pulling his baseball cap lower over his eyes and sauntering off in the direction of the harbour.

'Quickly,' Wei-Li urged Charlie, taking him by the arm.

He took one last glance up at the attic window, then set off with her, feeling just a little weak at the knees... He was pleased to see that whatever Kev had been up to, Rosebud's lock and door unlike the one in the vestry in Lanteglos church, were completely unmarked and intact.

'You say the attic, Charlie?' Mohan asked, directing his torch beam around the living room while they got their bearings.

'Yes.'

He removed a heavy bag that was slung over his shoulder and started to delve inside. 'Okay, but I'm going to set a camera up here. It will pick up any phenomena, and I'll angle it so we can keep an eye on the door in case anyone comes.'

'We're not going to have a light on are we?'

'Not needed,' said Wei-Li. 'We use night vision equipment.'

'Sounds expensive...'

He could just make out her grin in the low light. 'Having a rich dad does have its benefits!'

They left Mohan getting the camera ready, and went in search of the stairs. Charlie pulled his own torch out, but Wei-Li, who was guiding them with her own, cautioned him not to switch it on just yet.

'We don't want more light showing at the windows than necessary.'

They crept up to the next floor as quietly as they could on the bare wooden floorboards. The house was nearly empty, but Wei-Li's roving torch beam lit up a few items that had been left behind: a chair here, a little table with an empty plant pot on it there. But in the attic, the picture was very different.

To reach it, Charlie led Wei-Li up a very narrow, rickety staircase to a small door with an old-fashioned round metal knob. At first, when he tried to turn it the knob didn't yield and he thought it was locked. But when he tried again with a bit more effort the stiffness was overcome and it turned all the way. He switched his own torch on and scanned the attic room from the open doorway. To Charlie's surprise, this place was carpeted and furnished. It was as if the Victorian occupants had just popped out for a moment.

He was twitchy enough as it was, and the play of shadows as his beam probed the room gave the impression of something flitting about, hiding from the light. At least, he *hoped* that was the explanation. Unnerved, he switched the torch off almost without intending to.

'*Anything wrong*?' Wei-Li whispered.

He took a deep breath. 'No. I thought I saw something, but it must have been my torch.'

'Hadn't we better go in then?'

'Er, yes…'

Turning his torch back on, he felt his way into the attic as cautiously as if the floorboards beneath his feet were rotten. He could see now that it was quite a big room, running from the front of the house to the back. It felt colder in here, and there was a musty, mildewy smell in the air. There was an ancient mirror with mottled glass and a carved wooden frame on the wall to his right. A spectral cobweb formed a silky bridge between a battered armchair and a heavy wooden dining table. On the wall opposite the door was some sort of dresser. It was at least two metres high; the bottom half was a chest of drawers with candlesticks at either end, along with a few other ornaments and trinkets. The top half of was a series of shelves bearing plates, cups and more little knick-knacks, together with three framed photographs. Silvery spiders' webs draped everything, and particles of dust floated through the torch beam like miniature ice crystals on a frosty day.

And it did feel frosty. Charlie shivered, and pulled down the rolled-up sleeves of the top he was wearing.

Wei-Li came alongside him. 'A drop in temperature is a classic sign of…a *presence*.'

Charlie didn't even dare reply, as if his voice might alert the 'presence' to his intrusion.

Wei-Li risked switching her own torch on now.

'It's as if someone only moved out yesterday…'

She directed her beam towards the photographs on the middle shelf of the dresser. A large, rectangular one in the centre was flanked by two smaller square ones – and the one on the left looked familiar to Charlie. He forced himself to go deeper into the room, playing his own torchlight on it. It was a smaller version of the one in the Schooner pub, but without the writing beneath it.

'It's the man and boy who Cornelius Penhale saved.'

Wei-Li came to join him just as Mohan arrived and started unpacking his bag, plucking out a laptop, another camera, and some gadgets Charlie didn't recognise.

'But who are these?' she asked. Illuminated by her torch like actors in a theatre spotlight, the larger middle photograph showed a group of people packed together closely for the camera, but their images were so small it was almost impossible to make out individual faces. 'It looks like Polruan quay, but years and years ago…'

Charlie peered closer. 'You're right.' And he had an idea as to who the people were. 'Eight, nine, ten. Ten children and seven adults including the two crewmen. Wei-Li, these are the people who drowned – plus Isaac Trewin and William.'

Wei-Li gazed at the rows of blurred faces and sighed sadly. 'They must have been excited. The day before they were going to start new lives. Some of those kids are tiny…'

'But what's this?' Charlie had moved on to the third photograph. It was a solitary man from around the same period judging from his clothes – but his face had been blotted out by ink or something similar. Charlie suddenly felt unaccountably on edge, as if someone had crept up behind him, and had to turn away from the dresser. As he did so, his face became entangled in a cobweb, some strands clinging to the moistness of his open mouth. He let out a cry, spluttering and spitting.

'You will let the whole street know we're here!' Mohan hissed. He was studying the glowing screen of his laptop; the picture was split into four, showing different scenes, the view from the infrared cameras making each one look eerie. 'This is the first camera, in the living room facing the front door. Then we've got one in an empty room on the next floor, another on the landing facing the stairs, and finally I've put one in the corner of this room looking towards the window. All four are being recorded.'

'Do you want to try the EMF meter, Charlie?' Wei-Li asked.

'What's that?'

Mohan handed him a device like a big old-fashioned mobile phone, but with a row of coloured lights near the top. 'It's normally used by electricians to diagnose problems with wiring, but it's been discovered that they are sensitive to the presence of ghosts – and can even be used to communicate with them.'

Charlie took it from him with great reluctance, fearing it would start bleeping and flashing as soon as he touched it. But the black plastic object lay cold and inert in his hand.

'Look!' said Wei-Li, who had gone exploring further into the attic. Her torch was pointing at the floor.

'I can't see anything,' said Charlie.

'Exactly.' She moved her torch around as if tracing out the four sides of a large rectangle. 'Look how light the carpet is in the middle of the room compared to the outer edges.'

'Something was there for a long time,' Mohan said.

'*A rug*!' Charlie cried. 'It's got to be the one Henry Penhale took into his storeroom!'

Just as he leaned forwards to examine the floor, the EMF meter in his hand suddenly blinked into life. He dropped it as if it had given him an electric shock, and in the same instant there was a violent crash at the far end of the attic. He spun round just in time to see something bouncing off the wall near the door, and then a different dark shape sprang from the top of dresser, aiming right for him. Mohan shrieked, and Charlie dived to one side as the black thing hurtled silently over the carpet. Charlie curled up in a ball, waiting to be hit, possessed – he didn't know what.

But nothing happened.

He heard Mohan whimpering, and then Wei-Li's cool voice.

'It's a cat.'

It should have been funny, but no one was laughing. Charlie sat up and saw, illuminated in Wei-Li's torch beam, two striking green eyes a couple of metres away, staring right at him. He let out a long, grateful breath.

'Thank God! I thought it was…I don't know what I thought it was – but nothing good! It must have knocked something off the dresser.'

Wei-Li had gone to investigate, and was holding the picture that had the blacked-out face. 'This was on the floor – it's what made the first noise. The cat could have knocked it off…'

'But it flew across the room and hit the wall!' said Charlie.

'And how could a cat get in here anyway?' Mohan added. 'I made sure the front and back doors were shut before I came upstairs.'

'It was perhaps already locked in,' Charlie suggested.

The pair of emerald eyes stared unblinkingly, defiantly at

them.

Mohan tutted. 'I also checked every room.'

'Plus,' added Wei-Li, 'if it *had* been locked it would have been without food and water for who knows how long. It doesn't look starving to me.'

'Oh, no…' Mohan gasped, gazing at his laptop. Charlie could see the light from the screen – the only other illumination in the room besides their torches – rapidly dimming. 'Battery drain – but I fully charged it before we set off and it should last eight hours!'

Charlie felt even colder air on his face now, as if someone had opened a freezer door.

'Temperature drop,' Mohan cried, a hint of fear in his voice now. '*Something's going to happen.*'

At the same time, the EMF meter lying on the floor began to blink again – the red, orange and green lights flashing on and off rapidly, crazily.

'The cat!' said Wei-Li.

Charlie pulled his eyes away from the meter, and now the cat was at the other end of the room. Its eyes were fixed on a particular spot, it's back arched, fur raised. But when Charlie aimed his torch into that area there was nothing but the mirror on the wall reflecting his beam, and the cat hadn't been looking towards the mirror. There was a piercing yowl. He twitched his torch back to the cat and the beam mingled with Wei-Li's. It was spitting and hissing like some sort of demon, and seemed about ready to attack some unseen enemy.

Wei-Li screamed.

She shone her torch beam back on the mirror now – revealing a face.

It was a shimmering, contorted, malevolent face that Charlie recognised instantly. He let out a cry and instinctively grabbed Wei-Li's arm, seeing as he did so the madly dancing lights from the EMF meter reflected in her white sleeve.

Without warning the mirror jumped from the wall, shattering on the floor below even though it was thickly carpeted.

Mohan's laptop was dead. The EMF meter went blank. The cat let out another unearthly howl and sprang past them into the darkness as if on the attack. Charlie and Wei-Li instinctively swung their torches round to pick it out – but the second they did so, both their batteries failed. They were all in total darkness, listening to the furious hissing and yowling. Charlie could *sense* something despite his blindness. It was like the feeling in the air before a thunderstorm, an ominous sense of something about to happen, something powerful, something beyond human control or understanding.

And it was building rapidly.

He knew the others were aware of it too.

'*This is bad!*' cried Mohan. '*Very bad – grab everything and get out NOW!*'

twelve

Charlie cowered in East Street watching strange lights flashing and flickering in the attic window as if there was some sort of otherworldly disco going on. The sounds of crashing and banging seemed to make the whole house shake, and he couldn't believe it hadn't woken the whole village, yet no curtain twitched, no other lights came on.

What had they done? It felt like the end of the world. His legs buckled and he sank to the floor…

*

He sat upright, breathing hard and fast, heart pounding, barely aware of time passing. Then he became aware of early morning sunlight, softly diffused by pastel blue cotton curtains, bathing his face.

It took Charlie a few minutes to figure out where he was, what had been real and what had been a nightmare. Then he remembered that he had spent the night in one of Treffry House's numerous bedrooms. The décor was mostly a tranquil, pale blue, and a serene Buddha sat on top of a bookcase facing his bed. It was all very peaceful and pleasant – but when he noticed a small mirror above a dressing table, it brought the events of the previous night crashing back into his consciousness.

Why had he even gone there? What were they really hoping to achieve?

Whatever it was, all they seemed to have done was stir something up, something dark and dangerous that was better left alone.

He threw back the duvet and traipsed to the window. It overlooked the courtyard, and there was Wei-Li, practising her Tai Chi again with the grace of a ballet dancer, her black hair in a ponytail and the blue and gold silk costume glistening as if made of liquid. She looked so calm, controlled yet relaxed, yet he knew that even she had been scared last night.

He met up with Wei-Li and Mohan at breakfast in a spacious kitchen that had every modern appliance and gadget imaginable, mostly of shiny silver. It was like a space station. They had been perched on stools around a big central breakfast bar by Nina, the cook and cleaner. Wei-Li's father had left early, and she was busy making them a cooked breakfast. The mood was subdued, and there was little conversation at first. But Charlie needed at least a little reassurance.

'Surely it's not *always* like that when you carry out your investigations? If it is, I wish someone would have warned me…'

'Well,' Mohan mused, 'there was the time in Lostwithiel when we saw the shadow figure move across the landing and got an EVP saying *"Get out!"*.' As usual, he was glued to the screen of his beloved laptop.

'What's an EVP?'

'Electronic Voice Phenomenon. You can often catch paranormal voices on digital recorders that can't be heard by the human ear.'

'But, Mohan, that wasn't on the same scale as last night,' said Wei-Li.

He looked up from his computer and nudged his glasses up his nose with a spindly middle finger. Charlie thought even he, the one who thought it was all explainable by science, still looked somewhat traumatised by what had happened to them.

'No,' he admitted. 'No, it wasn't on the same scale at all…'

Wei-Li took a sip of orange juice. 'Someone tried to get through to me.'

'You mean like, psychically?' Charlie asked.

She nodded. 'But it was blocked by the anger of the man in the mirror, whoever he was. I don't think he meant to; it was just that his emotions were so strong it overpowered almost everything else. But I did hear—'

She stopped while Nina came over with their breakfasts, waiting until she went off to do some cleaning.

'I did hear…*something*. Like voices, especially children…but distant, and drowned out by the rage of the man in the mirror.'

Charlie felt his skin tingle. 'I thought I heard something like that when we took the boat out to Blackbottle Rock.'

Clouds swallowed the sun, casting Wei-Li's face into shadow. He noticed her eyes moistening.

'*So sad…* I couldn't hear the words but I picked up such terrible, terrible despair…'

'But what can we *do*? Why do you investigate cases like this unless you can *do* something?'

'They need to be released. They either don't realise they're dead and stay in the places they used to know, or they do realise but are trapped because of something unfinished, something that needs to be put right.'

'Or,' said Mohan, eyes glued to his laptop, '*they* are actually *it*. Trapped, yes – but negative energy that needs to be released from the surroundings.'

'It felt like *they* to me,' said Charlie. 'Anyway, what makes batteries suddenly die like ours did?'

'The theory is,' Mohan explained, 'that ghosts draw on the energy within batteries in order to make themselves visible, able to appear and interact with our world.'

'That's also why rooms get colder when a ghost is present,' Wei-Li added. 'They somehow make use of heat, which is a form of energy, in the same way.'

Outside, massing dirty grey clouds cast the kitchen into a murky half-light that somehow unnerved Charlie. He was glad when Wei-Li skipped over to switch a light on.

'I've got something! Mohan cried suddenly, the images on his screen reflecting in his glasses as he leaned closer for a better look.

'Are you going through the camera footage?'

'It's the one in the attic.'

They gathered around him expectantly, hunched over on his stool as he skipped back to whatever it was he'd seen and set the view to full-screen. Even with the camera's night vision ability, the dark images were grainy and indistinct, like a clip from the earliest days of black and white film. Even though the camera was a fixed and nothing was happening, the way it kept readjusting and refocusing to compensate for the lack of light created the illusion that things were moving about, and Charlie wondered whether Mohan was mistaken. Finally, though, something did happen. They could see the photograph shoot off the dresser, becoming a blur crossing the middle of the screen.

Charlie pulled a face. 'We saw that with our own eyes!'

'I *thought* I saw something else…' Wei-Li said hesitantly.

'*Look!*' Mohan urged, irritated. 'Look again – *closer*!'

Charlie and Wei-Li leaned on Mohan's shoulders, their faces beside his as he replayed the few seconds of footage again. And this time Charlie saw it too.

Almost camouflaged by the flickering shadows, a black shape moved quickly from right to left towards the dresser, with which it seemed to merge and then vanish. The instant it did so was when the picture flew off.

'*Play it again…*' he demanded.

Mohan ran it through several times, pausing and playing so they could examine every frame. And each time he did so, Charlie thought he could make out more of the figure swooping across the room.

And it was a figure. A human figure.

The edges of the shape were blurry and pixelated, but it was the silhouette of a man, leaning forward slightly as if in running posture. Charlie thought he could make out a long, black coat, and a black peaked cap was clearly visible. He shivered. It could only be one thing. Sharing the same eerie attic room with them that night had been a genuine ghost.

He pulled away from the screen and stared out of the window at the darkening skies outside, but Wei-Li was still glued to the screen.

'Play it one more time, Mohan,' she asked.

He sighed wearily. 'We've seen all we going to see. I mean, I know it's the best thing we've ever captured, but—'

'It's not the pictures I'm thinking of. Play it with the sound on max.'

He rolled his eyes. 'There *is* no audio with the cameras!'

'But…I heard something when you were looking at it earlier.'

'That must have been when I was going through what I caught on my digital recorder. But there are no EVPs – I've checked.'

'Just humour me.'

Making a big show of his reluctance, Mohan called up the audio file he'd loaded onto the laptop and clicked 'play'. There was a long period of silence punctuated by the occasional rustling and shuffling as they moved around the room. Eventually, Charlie heard the clatter of the photograph hitting the wall, followed a couple of minutes later by the smashing of glass as the mirror hit the floor. Then came Mohan's agitated voice: *'This is bad! Very bad – grab everything and get out NOW!'*

'I wasn't panicking,' he said hastily, swivelling round in his chair. 'I would like to point out that it's the policy of the FPI to abort a ghostwatch whenever the conditions indicate there might be danger to any member or—'

'Look,' said Wei-Li, pointing at the screen. 'It's still running. You were in such a panic – sorry, strategic withdrawal – that you forgot to turn it off. What I heard comes next.'

Charlie looked at the graphic, which was a bit like one of those hospital heart monitors, with peaks for sound and a flat-line for silence, and it clearly showed there were few seconds of the recording left to run.

'It's just our footsteps,' said Mohan.

He played it anyway, and all they could hear was the swishing of clothes and jumble of scurrying feet descending the stairs, quickly fading to nothing.

'That's when the battery dies,' Mohan explained.

But Wei-Li was still shaking her head. 'Have you got earphones for the laptop?'

'Not with me...'

'I think my music player ones will fit,' Charlie said, studying the port on the edge of the computer.

They did, and they watched Wei-Li's face intently as listened once more. She began to breathe more deeply, and then a tear emerged from the corner of one of her deep, dark eyes and trickled down her cheek. She took off the headset and handed it to Charlie, while Mohan played the last part of the file once again.

Just after Mohan's warning cry, as they were fleeing the attic room, he heard it. He had heard it before at – Blackbottle Rock. This time it was clearer.

Children, men, women.

Screaming...wailing...pleading.

Desperate voices, scattered on a roaring wind.

Worst of all, the pitiful screams of a terrified baby.

Charlie snatched the headphones off and threw them on to the table, blinking rapidly. He gazed at Wei-Li, and their tears seemed to mingle into one across the room.

thirteen

Charlie knew the Witch was watching his every move. Watching, waiting. Plotting to destroy him. Sitting at the back of the little ferry as it chugged and bobbed through the water from Fowey on its way to Polruan, he knew she would be able to see him directly from her lair right at this moment.

But the Witch wasn't there.

It was Sue.

Sue sitting by the window, writing post cards. Sue greeting him with a cheery smile. Sue asking him if he enjoyed his sleepover.

Somehow – Charlie didn't know how – the Witch had gone. Forever.

Even as he was waffling on about having a good time, making up some random stuff about playing computer games and listening to music, something was prompting him to tell her some or all of the truth. And then it dawned on him what that something was.

She would understand.

'Where's Dad?'

'He's popped to the store. We've run out of milk, and you know he can't do without his giant mugs of tea! I'm so glad you're getting on with your new friends…'

'Actually…' Charlie began hesitantly.

She seemed to pick up that he had something on his mind, and put her pen down to give him her full attention.

'Is everything all right, Chas?'

'No – well, it is, but… I saw a ghost last night.'

She didn't laugh. She didn't ask if he'd been up to no good. Her eyes were searching his to see if he was all right. Once he started, it all poured out; he told her everything and then watched anxiously for her reaction. She looked shocked. Well, maybe not shocked, but it certainly took her a minute or two to take it all in.

'Charlie, it's the kind of scary but exciting thing I wish had happened to me when I was your age, but this sounds like serious stuff and the sensible grown-up part of me is worried. You can understand that, can't you?'

He nodded. 'But Wei-Li says these spirits need to be released – that's what the FPI do. Although it was frightening, now, in a funny way, I don't think it was dangerous. More sad than anything.'

'So what's the plan?'

'We still believe Henry Penhale is tied up in it in some way or knows something. We're going to...er...investigate that a bit more, later today.'

She gave a crooked smile. 'I take it that the details of the plan are for *FPI eyes only*?'

'Kind of. But it includes another ghostwatch tonight. Not midnight or anything, but after dark.'

'I'm sure I can take it as read that you'll be careful...'

'Course!'

'And that you'll get out if anything dodgy starts to happen. And you'll take your mobile and ring me if—'

'*Promise!*'

She relaxed a little. 'Well, you might not share all of the FPI's secrets with me, but speaking of Penhale I've got something to share with you.'

On the table next to the post cards was a plum-coloured folder. She opened it and pulled out what looked like a photocopy of an old newspaper article.

For Sale by Candle at Lloyd's Coffee House in Lombard St, on Wednesday July 29th at twelve noon: Five Hogsheads of Madeira Wine of the most superior sort, twenty casks of fine French Brandy, all newly transported from the Continent and salvaged unspoilt from the foundered lugger Rosebud, *Fowey.*

'Cornelius Penhale's boat,' Charlie commented. 'What does sale by candle mean?'

'It's a type of auction. A bit like eBay, but instead of the computer counting down the time they lit a candle, and the bidding ended the second it burned itself out. But don't you see the significance of it?'

'Not really. They saved some booze – but it doesn't mention anything about Cornelius Penhale or Isaac Trewin who had the gravestones made – or *anyone*.'

'But the booze is the thing! Taxes on alcohol from abroad were sky-high then, which was why there was a lot of smuggling. It would have been worth an awful lot of money.'

'Yes – Cornelius probably wanted to replace the *Rosebud*, so I suppose he needed it. But I still don't see—'

'The ship was heading for the rocks, where it was smashed to pieces – wooden barrels aren't going to survive that. They *had* to have been unloaded before the boat went down.'

Charlie felt himself turning pale. '*Cornelius Penhale saved his precious wine and left the people to drown!*'

'I can't think of any other explanation. What Trewin had to do with it, and why he was saved, I have no idea. Maybe that's for the FPI to find out!'

Charlie fell into a trance-like state as he tried to work out how it all fitted together, but Dad's return cut it short.

'I got us some more chocolate for this evening!' he announced breezily.

'Ah…' began Sue. 'Charlie's going to be out again tonight…'

Dad's angular frame sagged a little. 'Aww…'

'But it's not a sleepover,' she added, giving Charlie a meaningful look. 'He'll be out for an hour or two with his new friends, then back here.'

Charlie nodded eagerly.

'What are you up to this time?' Dad didn't sound annoyed, just curious.

'Astronomy,' Sue blurted out. 'They've got a telescope, and they're going to identify some constellations.'

'Sounds great! In fact, *I* wouldn't mind tagging along—'

'*NOOO*!' Charlie and Sue cried in unison, then both looked at each other and burst out laughing.

'Well, I only asked…' said Dad.

'Sorry,' Sue explained, 'but it's a well-known fact that dads aren't allowed to go gate-crashing kids' adventures – especially on holiday. Besides, it means more chocolates for us!'

He shrugged. 'Go and have your adventure – but I want a go of that telescope before we go home.'

'Thanks.' Charlie addressed them both, but he managed to give Sue the faintest hint of a conspiratorial smile.

*

Charlie was more nervous about The Plan than he was about the ghostwatch.

They had carefully worked it out and even rehearsed it before he'd left Treffry House that morning. It all seemed fine in theory, but the real thing would require nerve and split-second timing. He dreaded to think what might happen if The Plan went wrong. All he knew was he would be the one in trouble if it did.

Heavy clouds scudded overhead on a stiff breeze, as if trying to race the ferry bringing Wei-Li and Mohan across. Every now and then Charlie felt tiny spots of rain on his face, but then it would blow over just as quickly. The faces of his two friends were taut and solemn when they greeted him.

'Is he on his own?' Mohan asked.

'Yes – there's no assistant working in the Beachcomber as far as I can see,' Charlie informed them.

'So we wait,' said Wei-Li, settling down on a bench that

provided a good view of the shop. 'You take up your position, Charlie, and the second Henry Penhale goes into his store for something, I'll put my hat on.'

She opened her bag to show him a glimpse of the yellow baseball cap. With a quick dip of his head to show he understood, Charlie crossed the quay and sat on the low harbour wall outside the Lugger pub. He was close enough to be able to nip round the corner and up the steps to the Beachcomber's storeroom in seconds, yet positioned so he couldn't be seen by Penhale as he moved from one place to the other.

It was a long wait. They had no idea when – or even if – Henry Penhale would need to go to his store. Charlie began to feel self-conscious, sitting in the same spot for so long. Eventually, fidgeting around on the concrete wall to get rid of 'numb bum' syndrome wasn't enough, and he had to get up and walk around a bit – while making sure to keep an eye on Wei-Li and Mohan for the signal.

But it never came. An hour passed, and Charlie could see Mohan, who in his boredom had been playing about with his phone, his music player and every other gadget he had with him, talking earnestly to Wei-Li. Charlie didn't need Wei-Li's psychic powers to know that he was fed up and wanted to either call it off or try a new plan. He decided to take matters into his own hands, and left his post to go over and discuss it with them.

'Tell her this is ridiculous!' Mohan said imploringly when Charlie arrived, no doubt hoping he would back him up. 'We should have come up with a plan to get his storeroom unlocked then create a diversion. We could have just got Kev to unlock it!'

'It's a bit late for that!' Wei-Li insisted. 'We knew it could take a long time. That rug was taken from Rosebud Cottage for a reason. It could be the key to this whole business!'

Charlie suddenly felt like a referee.

'It's nearly lunchtime anyway. Maybe we just ought to get a bite to eat and come back later. He goes into the storeroom more than once in a day, so even if we miss one time we'll get him the next.'

'Yes,' parroted Mohan. 'We ought to have a break and come back later.'

Charlie could see Wei-Li knew she was out-voted.

'Just a short break, then. But this is so important that I really think—'

'Hang on…' Mohan cut in, looking beyond her. '*He's out*!'

Charlie spun round, and there was little Henry Penhale with his snooty, upturned nose and thick glasses, today wearing a ridiculous pink jumper. He strode towards the steep steps leading up to the store as if he owned Polruan.

As soon as he had his back to them, Wei-Li cried, '*Back to your position and look for the signal, Charlie*!'

Charlie ran across the quay, passing within feet of Penhale as he went up the outside staircase, and disappeared round the corner. There were two phases of this plan where things could go very wrong, and the first one was coming up. It was frustrating not to be able to see it happening, but he knew that at this very moment Mohan would be approaching Henry Penhale and telling him there was an emergency in the shop. At the same time, Wei-Li would slip into Beachcomber and pretend to faint. But would Penhale believe Mohan, or might he simply stay put? If he did return to the shop, would he spot Wei-Li running in?

Things moved fast now.

Only seconds after he'd got back to his post, he saw Wei-Li put her yellow hat on then immediately hurry out of sight towards the shop. Charlie made his move, and as soon as he turned the corner he saw Penhale huffing and puffing back to the Beachcomber. Mohan must have been convincing. He now took up a position where he could see both the shop and the storeroom, ready to phone Charlie if Penhale came back early. Without hesitating, Charlie ran up the steps two at a time. His heart sank when he saw the door was closed. Had Penhale locked it?

To his relief, the handle turned freely. He quickly slipped in and closed the door behind him, fumbling in the darkness for a light switch. As he did so, he thought he heard a faint sound coming from somewhere inside the store and froze. But all was silent, and within seconds he'd found the switch. The sudden flood of bright light made him blink. He was surprised at how small the storeroom actually was – but at least there was no possibility of anyone else hiding in here, so the noise must have been in his imagination. Tall shelves lined both walls, and piles of boxes of crisps, confectionery and other stuff formed a row down the centre that was taller than Charlie. It was cramped and stuffy, barely room to move about, let alone hide a big heavy rug. Where could it be? He scanned the shelves, the gloomy corners of the room, and he was creeping towards the far end when his foot caught something.

It was the edge of the rug, sticking out from the gap beneath the bottom shelf. Charlie dropped to his knees and pulled it out, and there was just enough room to unroll half of it. It just looked like an ordinary rug. Ancient and faded, but the kind of thing you'd see on the floor of any old house. There was some sort of swirling green pattern on a deep red background that just might contain a clue or even code, but there was no time to study it. All he could do was stick to the plan and take pictures on his phone to study later. He got a few images from the first half of the rug, then wrestled with the cumbersome thing so he could reveal the other. As he grunted and struggled, there was a sudden tearing sound and Charlie stopped, staring in horror at the gaping hole he'd made. His fingers hadn't gone right through – it was just a rip in the backing of the rug, but a pretty obvious one that Henry Penhale was bound to see if he decided to look at the underside for any reason. Just how valuable was this thing, anyway?

But as he pulled his fingers out, they brushed against the edge of something, something that rustled like paper. He tentatively probed with his index finger, and examining the hole more closely he saw to his relief that he *hadn't* caused the rip himself. It was a small, neat cut that must have been made with a sharp knife then glued back down so neatly that it would have been easy to miss. He reached further inside, and pulled out a folded piece of paper. It was yellow with age and fragile, and writing showed through from the inside.

Just as he carefully began to unfold it, his phone's ringtone shattered the silence and nearly gave him a heart attack.

Henry Penhale was on his way back – but Charlie hadn't photographed the rest of the rug or the note.

Then he heard it again.

Not his phone, but the same faint sound he'd heard when he'd first entered. He was still on his hands and knees, and when he raised his head he was face-to-face with the black cat.

Those familiar, chilling green eyes bored into his, and a sinister noise came from the back of its throat, starting low and quietly but rapidly building in pitch and intensity, until finally the creature let out a spine-chilling screech and leapt at him. Charlie rolled to evade it, then scrambled and stumbled out of the storeroom, leaving the rug where it was, the door open. Despite his blind panic, he had time to puzzle over something: any cat had to be way faster than he was – so why had he felt no thud as it hit him, no clawing at his legs? Come to that, how could it even have been in there?

As he clattered to the bottom of the steps, he caught a flash of pink out of the corner of his eyes, and knew Penhale had turned the corner. Had he seen him? Was it obvious where he'd just been?

Right at that moment, Charlie didn't care.

fourteen

'This place is also haunted,' said Mohan casually.

'Let's deal with one set of ghosts at a time if you don't mind…'

Charlie shuffled uncomfortably, surveying the half-ruined stone walls of the Blockhouse, the little fortress that used to guard the entrance to the harbour. The external structure was still largely intact, but here inside the roof was open to the skies and the heavy, ominous clouds that hung over them.

'Do you think he saw me?'

'Didn't look like it to me,' said Wei-Li. 'He was in such a hurry to get back to his store-room that he didn't seem to be aware of anything around him. He almost knocked an old man over in his rush.'

'But he will, of course, know that *someone* was in the store – and that they found the rug,' Mohan pointed out.

'What we don't know is whether he knew about the letter hidden inside it,' said We-Li.

Mohan tutted. 'Of *course* he does. That's why he stole the rug from Rosebud Cottage and hid it!'

But Charlie wasn't so sure. 'The cut in the lining of the rug ran along the line of the thread. It was almost invisible, and it didn't look or *feel* like it had been opened in a long time. If he knew it existed, he's had plenty of time to get at it.'

'*Ahem…*' Mohan coughed theatrically. 'Am I the only one who would like to find out what's actually *in* the letter?'

'Oh, right…' Charlie fished it out of his pocket.

'*Careful!*' Wei-Li cautioned. 'It looks really delicate.'

She was right. A slight crack had begun to open up along one of the fold lines despite his gentle handling. It was a roughly A4 sized sheet of paper, so thin you could almost see through it. Neat but spidery handwriting in black ink that had faded to a muddy brown filled the page. It took Charlie some time to get used to the way certain letters were formed, but after studying it for a minute or two he was ready to read it out to the others.

I, Isaac James Trewin, along with my son William, am the sole survivor of the wreck of the lugger Rosebud, and this is my True Account of that Fateful Day. The vessel departed Fowey on the 17th of April 1856 for London. On board were the following besides myself and my son: EDWARD & SARAH EDGECOMBE & their four children; JOSIAH & HANNAH SMITH & their five children (including PRUDENCE – but a Babe in Arms); JOHN VERCOE & NATHANIEL HAWKE (crewmen). In addition, the boat carried a large cargo of wines to be sold at our destination.

No sooner had we cleared Saint Catherine's Point than the wind backed and increased in violence, putting us in great peril. Onlookers observing our progress from Saint Saviour's Point immediately sent word to the Rosebud's owner, Cornelius Penhale Esquire, who put out in a gig rowed by several of his stoutest men.

The squall quickly passed, but it had done its damage to the mast and sails of Rosebud and forced us close on a lee shore, namely that part of the coast known as Blackbottle Rock, such that it was impossible to work our way off despite the best efforts of all. On coming alongside, Mr Penhale demanded that his valuable Cargo be transferred before any Christian souls. Yes, even women and children. Such was the distress of those in our sinking vessel that some tried to board the gig forcibly, but were pushed back on the orders of Mr Penhale.

I, to my shame, offered Cornelius Penhale all of the considerable monies promised me by an uncle to commence business in London, if he would but permit myself and my son to board the gig. This, with bad grace, he finally agreed to. We were saved along with the cargo just before the boat hit Blackbottle Rock and disappeared beneath the waves, but never shall I forget the distressing sights and sounds I witnessed that day.

My conscience later obliged me to inform the people of Polruan of the true circumstances of my rescue. Mr Penhale, in a panic that he would be hounded out of the area if not lynched, offered to not only to forget the money I had promised him, but to pay me a considerable sum to gain my silence. Once more I weakened. I did, however, spend much of the money on gravestones for those who perished.

Every night in my dreams I see the faces and hear the voices of those died, and I am determined that one day the truth, particularly concerning Mr Cornelius Penhale – as heartless and wicked a man who ever lived – should be known by all.

Signed this day, 11th of April 1856
Isaac Trewin

For a second Charlie thought he heard the cries of the drowning people again, but it was only the wind on the water and the squabbling of distant gulls.

'The conditions indicate the coming of a storm,' Mohan announced.

'We've just learned the truth about Penhale and why his old house is haunted, and all you can talk about is the weather!'

'It's just his way,' said Wei-Li. 'He does feel things deep down.'

A ragged flash of lightning far out to sea, framed by the small rectangular window of the Blockhouse, caught Charlie's eye. It was so far away that he heard no accompanying thunder.

'So what do we do – tell Henry Penhale we know the truth?'

'It's possible *he* doesn't know,' Mohan pointed out.

'I'm sure he does,' Wei-Li said. 'Otherwise why steal the rug? Why sneak around in Rosebud Cottage when it doesn't belong to his family anymore? If he doesn't know the whole story, he must at least know some of it. We need to concentrate on releasing those poor trapped souls.'

'But how?' Charlie asked. He remembered the horrors of last night, and wasn't at all sure he wanted to hear what she might suggest.

'Just stick to the plan. We go to Rosebud Cottage again tonight.'

'I'm no expert, but no matter how haunted a place is, ghosts don't come on demand or appear every day. I've only got a few days left in Polruan – what if nothing happens?'

'These things can't be hurried,' said Mohan.

'Can't you kind of *summon them up*, Wei-Li?'

She shook her head. 'I'm sensitive to them when they appear, but I can't make them come. We'll just have to hope for the best.'

'And that all our batteries don't die like last time,' Mohan added.

Charlie just wanted to free the souls of those poor children and didn't care about the batteries. Batteries were easy to replace, and if the ghosts drained them in order to materialise, who was he to…

Then it hit him.

'Hang on… You said ghosts make use of energy, like the heat in a room and the power from batteries, so they can take physical form…'

'That's the theory,' Mohan replied.

'What if we *give* them the power they need?!'

'What do you mean?' asked Wei-Li.

'Why don't we take everything with a battery in we can lay our hands on? They almost appeared when we had just a few gadgets. If we take loads of them, surely all that battery power would be enough. We can help to send them into the light or whatever it is you do!'

Mohan's eyebrows shot up. 'I never thought of that…'

'It's risky,' Wei-Li warned.

'How?' Charlie demanded. 'It might be scary, but we *want* to make contact.'

'We want to make contact with specific people, but they aren't the only spirits around. It would be like opening your front door and inviting everyone in everyone who passes by – not all of them are going to be friendly.'

Charlie sagged physically and mentally. He knew she was right and the thought of what might happen unnerved him, yet he hated the thought of going home and leaving things unfinished.

'Well, I'm in favour,' Mohan said firmly.

'This isn't a fascinating experiment,' said Wei-Li. 'This is real paranormal stuff. Real danger...' She glanced Charlie's way. 'But...if I'm out-voted, I'll go along with it.'

'Thanks,' said Charlie.

'But only on the condition that if I sense things are getting out of hand, we call a halt to it.'

Charlie nodded without hesitation.

'It depends on your definition of "out of hand", of danger...' Mohan began – but when he saw Charlie and Wei-Li glowering at him, he reluctantly gave in.

'So tonight it is then,' said Wei-Li, rising to go. 'But remember, we don't know what sort of things he might unleash – things I might not be able to control.'

As he watched them leave, Charlie saw lightning snake low over an inky sea once more, its tentacles spreading as if seeking something on the surface. A distant headland seemed to blink into existence and then was gone. This time, far-off thunder did rumble faintly but ominously across the water. It sounded like a warning.

fifteen

The river was dead calm, but it was an uneasy stillness. Angry blue-black clouds forged towards them, tumbling one on top of another like stampeding bulls. They seemed to squash the very air down, making it thick and heavy. It wasn't that late, and on other days it had still been light at this time, but it was as dark as midnight when the lights of the Polruan ferry appeared out of the gloom carrying Wei-Li, Mohan and Kev.

They spoke few words as they trooped to Rosebud Cottage, where Kev quickly and skilfully worked his magic on the lock once more before disappearing. This time, they armed themselves with an array of battery-powered devices. Each had laptop bags slung over the shoulder, and Charlie knew that, like him, their pockets were crammed with music players, new and old mobile phones, extra torches, still and video cameras. Mohan had an iPad, while Wei-Li had another sort of tablet and Charlie had borrowed Sue's own similar device. Shared between them were also digital voice recorders and Mohan's 'Ghost busting' kit: EMF meters, motion sensors and digital thermometers to record sudden drops in temperature.

A lot of battery power.

Enough to wake the dead…

Charlie had a sick feeling in his stomach, and almost wished he was leaving with Kev. But he knew he would never be able to forget the cries of those, especially the children, who drowned at Blackbottle Rock. He would never forgive himself if he left Polruan without trying to do something for them.

The first fat drops of rain splatted onto the street as Wei-Li led them inside, and almost as soon as Charlie closed the door behind him he heard the downpour quickly intensify, rattling like marbles off the roofs and windows all along East Street. They climbed the broad main staircase to the next floor, following Wei-Li's torch beam as it pierced the gloomy interior of the empty house and led them to the narrower, more claustrophobic steps to the attic. Charlie's legs felt heavy, reluctant to carry him into that black hole above his head; but he took a deep breath and pushed himself on. When Wei-Li opened the attic door, a gust of air wafted against Charlie's face: stale, humid and uninviting.

They filed into the eerie space, its Victorian furniture and decor picked out randomly as the torchlight searched the room.

To Charlie's surprise, though, it felt just as any other long-deserted room might once he was inside. There was no sense of 'presence' or foreboding – with all this old stuff, it was more like being in a museum after closing time. As he took out the different gadgets he'd brought along he remembered what Wei-Li had said about ghosts appearing when they wanted to, not when the living demanded it. After all the tension and nerves, he began to wonder whether this might all come to nothing, that it was daft to think you could summon ghosts just by having a few devices hanging around.

'Do you think we should arrange the things all around the room so that we've got every area covered?' Wei-Li asked in a hushed voice.

Mohan thought for a moment. The strange shadows on his face cast by the torchlight made it look as spooky as any ghost's. 'The whole idea of bringing all this stuff is to get a concentration of power, so we ought to have everything in one place.' He switched his own torch on and searched the room until settling on a heavy settee up against one wall.

'There.'

Charlie slipped the laptop bag off his shoulder and took the computer out. He and the others proceeded to arrange all of their devices on the settee, until very soon it looked like a shelf in a technology store.

'Shall we turn them on?'

'Not just yet,' said Wei-Li. 'Let's just take a minute to settle down and get the mood of the place.'

'Places don't have moods,' Mohan countered. 'They're just places. Bricks, wood, windows. I don't see why we shouldn't get started.'

Mohan bored Charlie at times, and as the two of them bickered, his attention drifted – until he saw something that that shouldn't have been possible.

He had been looking at the far end of the attic with his back to the window – yet he had just seen the reflected image of a flash of lightning outside. And that brief flicker of light had allowed him to see what had caused the reflection.

He lit up his torch, praying he would be proved wrong. But no, it was the mirror. The same mirror, with its mottled old glass and carved wooden frame that had leapt off the wall – that had landed on thick carpet yet had been smashed to pieces.

By now, Wei-Li and Mohan had noticed too.

'*It can't be*!' Mohan cried, marching down the room.

'Careful…' Wei-Li urged, following hesitantly in his footsteps.

But Mohan went right up to it. 'It must be a joke…a trick. Someone has bought an identical one.'

He ran the tips of his finger over the glass and frame, lifted it from the wall, checked the hook and wire it was hanging from. Charlie flashed his light around the faded old carpet beneath it, expecting to see at least the glint of small pieces of broken glass. There was nothing. Then he remembered the photograph that had flown across the room, and there it was on the dresser.

'The picture didn't break so maybe someone could have put it back, but the mirror…'

A low grumble of thunder filled the air outside.

'It's getting closer – I was counting the time since we saw the lightning.'

Typical, thought Charlie. *We're in a haunted house with weird things happening, and all he can think about it is calculations and scientific stuff.*

'I don't want to seem wimpy or anything,' he said, unable to take his eyes of the mirror, 'but is it all right if we turn it to face the wall?'

'Mirrors are known to be a way for spirits to pass from their world to ours – and that's what we want to happen tonight…' Wei-Li began. But she seemed to pick up on how much it was getting to him, and she reached up and carefully turned it so that only its back was showing. Then she walked to the brighter area of carpet, where the rug had once been.

Wei-Li closed her eyes and began to breathe deeply and rhythmically. Charlie felt himself tensing, waiting for something to happen. A faint rustling sound from behind made him spin round – but it was Mohan, using the bottom edge of his T-shirt to clean his glasses. Typical.

'I just don't sense anything,' Wei-Li said at last.

'Then it's time to switch everything on,' Mohan announced eagerly.

Again, Charlie felt a powerful, sickening tingling sensation sweeping through his body, threatening to engulf him – but he was determined to grit his teeth and see this through. He joined Mohan and Wei-Li at the sofa and they went through all the devices one by one, flicking them into life to the accompaniment of an assortment of beeps and flashing lights. The newly activated array of modern technology seemed completely out of place in this Victorian living room trapped in time.

All three of them stood tense and motionless, listening, watching. At first, Charlie could hardly breathe, expecting something terrifying to happen any second. But as the minutes passed, Charlie didn't need Wei-Li's psychic abilities to recognise that the atmosphere showed no signs of changing at all. It was stuffy and muggy because of the storm and every so often thunder echoed along East Street, but that was just weather, and he began to feel ridiculous. It was all his idea, and here they were staring at computers and music players expecting ghosts to leap out of them somehow.

'I did say you can't force these things...' remarked Wei-Li kindly.

'In theory, it was a good idea Charlie,' Mohan added. 'I'm surprised I didn't think of it first. Ghosts *do* make use of the energy from battery-powered devices. It's well known in ghost hunting circles.'

It seemed they were on the verge of giving up, and Charlie felt crushed. In three days he would be slumped in the back of the car on the long journey home, nothing accomplished, not even sure whether he would ever come back here. In his mind he heard the heart-rending screams of terrified children and parents calling their names, trying to reach them, trying to save them. For a moment he was back in the little boat off Blackbottle Rock, but now the cries were being drowned out by Henry Penhale's smug pronouncements about his 'hero' ancestor. *Why?* Why did he tell those lies? How long had he known the truth?

He shoved his hands in his pockets and scuffed his toe tetchily against the faded old carpet.

'*What was that*?' Mohan asked in an urgent whisper.

'Sorry – it was me,' Charlie admitted.

'No,' Wei-Li insisted, alert eyes darting around the room. 'I heard you, but there was something else...'

And now Charlie heard it, too. A creaking sound as if someone was pacing the floor somewhere in the house, every now and then stopping and listening, then moving on. He tried to probe the blackness of the room, but couldn't make out where it was coming from. His torch picked out the mirror with its back still facing outwards, the photo was still in its place on the dresser. But the noise started again, and was now getting quicker.

It was footsteps – and they were coming up the stairs.

Charlie felt naked, defenceless. How did you protect yourself from a ghost? He wanted to help the victims of the Blackbottle Rock disaster, but what he had witnessed here had seemed angry, powerful. Did they take their rage out on anyone who happened to be in their presence?

A dark shape appeared in the doorway.

Charlie could feel its eyes on him. His legs felt rubbery, but he was ready to run all the same. He tried to tell himself ghosts weren't solid – you could run right through them if you really had to…

'*What are you doing in my house?*'

Henry Penhale stepped into the light from Wei-Li's torch. The beam reflected eerily off his glasses, making his eyes invisible.

'It's not your house – you sold it,' Mohan said defiantly.

'You still have no right to be here. How did you get in? This was my family's home for generations and *I* have a key.'

'I bet the owners in London don't know you've still got one though,' Charlie challenged him.

For a moment Penhale hesitated, and Charlie knew he must be right. 'You're all trespassing. I'll make sure your parents know – and the police if necessary. *You* will have no defence, but I'll easily be able to explain away why I needed to pop into my old family home.'

'And will you be able to explain away why you stole the rug or tore the page out of the parish register?'

Charlie tried to sound cool, but he was shaking. It was partly anger at how the Creep kept up his lies about the Blackbottle Disaster and Cornelius Penhale's part in it, and partly fear at standing up to an adult like this.

To his amazement, his words seemed to hit their mark. Penhale's expression softened and he smiled sheepishly. He drew closer to them.

'Look, you youngsters appear to have done some splendid detective work, but you've got it all wrong…'

Charlie wasn't taken in by his sudden friendliness – but if it got them out of this tricky situation he wasn't too bothered by it either

'The rug actually *does* belong to me – it was something we never got round to taking out when we sold the place. I just happened to remember it, decided it would be nice to have a reminder of my illustrious ancestor—'

'*Illustrious*?' Mohan cried incredulously.

Penhale maintained his even temper. 'Oh, you've heard some of the older folk and their stories, have you? Well I can promise you they're all wrong – quite wrong! No one knows the history of Polruan – including the story of the Blackbottle Rock disaster – as well as I do. I've made it my life's work. There was a story put about by Isaac Trewin's family that Cornelius Penhale was some sort of villain, but I can only assume they were jealous of my ancestor. They wanted Trewin to be the hero and did it by attacking Cornelius, but I can assure you…'

The instant Henry Penhale uttered those words, Charlie noticed a flickering behind the man's head. Catching Charlie's gaze, Penhale broke off and turned. There was a vague play of faint light at the far end of the attic, like a candle flame seen through a net curtain. Was it a Charlie's imagination, or was it very slowly getting bigger, brighter? Wei-Li had spotted it too, and Charlie saw a look of concern darken her face. But Penhale was more intent on telling his story.

'It's understandable that Trewin's family should have felt that way. Petty jealousies flare up all the time in little places like this where everyone knows each other. And, with the best will in the world, stories get twisted and warped as the years pass by. Rest assured, children – Isaac Trewin and his son were lucky that Cornelius Penhale arrived to save the day…'

He must have thought that just because they were kids they were also idiots. The more he droned on with his stupid story, the more Charlie fumed.

But he was becoming aware that the anger wasn't just inside him.

It was outside too. It was building within the room.

The already heavy atmosphere was rapidly growing thicker, more stifling. It reminded him of diving to the bottom of the deep end of a swimming pool: pressure on his body, on his lungs, his eardrums. But it was more than merely physical. It was as if the room itself was raging against Penhale's words, and it was a fury that was building rapidly…

'*The mirror*!' Mohan cried, silencing Penhale in mid-flow.

Charlie gasped. It was facing the room again, reflecting the blinking lights from the devices on the sofa. But there was something else in the background – existing in the mirror, yet not a reflection of anything in the room. The vague light they'd seen earlier was growing, taking shape. A swirling mass with distorted features was gradually forming: nose, mouth. Charlie knew it was the wrathful face he had seen at the attic window. There were two red pinpoints that Charlie had thought were the reflections of lights on one of their devices. But as the face became clearer he saw that they were eyes, burning with rage, searing right into Charlie's heart. And then the screams began.

They were indistinct at first, like the wind whistling down the chimney, through the gaps in the old window frames – but with an undertone of frantic wails of desperation and despair.

For a moment Charlie had forgotten about Penhale, but now he saw the man twisting away from the image in the mirror, pressing his hands to his face. Even in the darkness, Charlie could see his whole body quivering.

'*Trewin!*' he gasped. '*It's Isaac Trewin*!'

The face shimmered and shifted as if made of smoke, but its features were fully formed now. The burning eyes searched the room like lasers, then fixed on Henry Penhale. He let out a strangled cry and made a sudden dash for the attic door. At the same moment, the vague ghostly voices became a storm of sound, filling the room, painful to the ears. It was carried on a wind as if from a storm at sea. It blew through the room, sending things flying, forcing Penhale away from the door.

Charlie covered his ears, wincing at the din. Rising above it all, he heard Wei-Li's cry.

'It's the mirror. It's all coming from the mirror!'

Its glass rippled as if made of water, and Trewin's face started to billow outwards, into the room. A body began to form around it. The shrieking intensified, and the lights on the machines blinked out one by one until only Trewin's red eyes remained. Charlie was cowering in a corner now, wanting to hide his face in his hands but unable to look away.

Then a flash of lightning seemed to reach in through the window like a jagged, silver knife. Charlie heard the hiss of static electricity, and felt his hair rise as if someone were holding a balloon over it.

'The power!' Charlie heard Mohan shout above the chaos. *'They're using all the power we brought – and now the electrical storm! THIS IS DANGEROUS!'*

But there was no escape. The wall of sound pressing on them, sucking the air out of the room.

And now figures began to appear beneath the mirror around Trewin's growing form. Fuzzy, misty shapes but clearly human. They rose and fell, gyrated, flailing arms, clutching hands – and Charlie knew what it reminded him of. Bodies thrashing in deep water.

He stuck his fingers in his ears, praying for it to end. Mohan and Penhale were recoiling too – but not Wei-Li.

To Charlie's astonishment, she actually took a step towards the chaos, ignoring the wind tearing at her clothes and hair. Facing her loomed the tall figure of Isaac Trewin, fully emerged from the mirror, a dark, menacing, shimmering shape circled by whirling, grasping figures. Wei-Li was looking right into Trewin's fiery eyes. She looked calm, her body relaxed but primed as if she were about to begin practising Tai Chi.

'*Only you can stop this*,' she called to Penhale.

'*I can't! I can't!*' he jabbered, his face buried in his hands.

'You know the truth. You can put an end to all the years of lies. You can't bring the dead back to life, but you can make sure that the truth about the way they died comes out. *Stop living a lie!*'

When Wei-Li spoke these last words, her voice changed. It became deeper, and her face took on an eerie darker, shadowy look.

'*We were both guilty, Cornelius and me*,' she continued – but now it was not her voice at all but that of a man in torment. '*But Cornelius let those people drown. A murderer in all but name. THEIR STORY MUST BE KNOWN!*'

'*Oh, God...*' Penhale sobbed, broken, defeated. '*I wanted to admit it but I couldn't. The family name...*' The reeling figures circled him now, clutching at his clothes. '*I can't carry the burden any longer. Please – I'll do anything, I'll tell everyone.*' His voice suddenly rose above the nightmarish cacophony filling the room. '*CORNELIUS PENHALE LET THEM DROWN TO SAVE HIS PRECIOUS CARGO.*'

As soon as he said this Wei-Li sank to her knees, looking drained but back to her old self. The unearthly noise ceased so abruptly that the silence itself seemed painful to Charlie's ears. Trewin and the swirling figures quickly began to lose their shape, drifting back towards the mirror until they finally dissolved into a cloudy mass, which was sucked into the dull glass. Then came the final act in the drama. The mirror shattered into a thousand pieces that rained down onto the carpet.

Charlie felt the heaviness in the room evaporate. He could breathe, his spirit felt unaccountably light. Climbing to his feet, he saw the storm clouds departing, revealing glittering stars and a rising crescent moon.

Mohan had removed his glasses and was rubbing his eyes as if he'd just woken from a deep sleep, and Henry Penhale simply stared blankly at the space where the mirror had hung. Wei-Li, in the middle of the room, rose slowly and brushed strands of long black hair, damp with sweat, from her face. Charlie saw tears in her eyes – but she was smiling at him. She was feeling it too.

They had released the ghosts of Blackbottle Rock.

sixteen

'I've known the truth for a few years,' said Henry Penhale. They had gathered in the kitchen of Rosebud Cottage before heading home. Charlie thought he looked older, the lines on his forehead deeper. All his old smugness and arrogance had gone, and he even seemed somehow smaller.

'And if I'm honest I'd guessed at it long before that. I'd heard the rumours from locals whose grandparents had been alive at the time – but they weren't keen to go into detail and I wasn't keen to hear any. Cornelius Penhale was a local hero whose story helped bring tourists to Polruan, and well, I enjoyed playing the local celebrity: giving my talks and guided tours, having newspaper and television people approaching me…'

'But you can still do that,' said Wei-Li. 'Polruan and Fowey have lots of interesting history.'

His face brightened. 'You're right. I suppose it was more about *me*. He was my ancestor. I wanted to share his fame.'

'So why did you steal the page from the burial register?' Charlie asked.

Penhale smiled ruefully. 'Ah – you're to blame for that. You and your mother.'

'She's not my mother,' he shot back a little more eagerly than he'd meant to.

'Oh, sorry. Well, Sue contacted me out of the blue – an author wanting to write a book about the Blackbottle Rock disaster. I panicked. No one had ever gone digging into the historical records – they'd always come to me, accepted my version. I was especially worried because a few weeks previously I'd discovered a little note scrawled in Isaac Trewin's hand on the back of the page that had the burial entries for the victims. He had secretly scrawled it there, probably near the end of his life, in the hope that it would be discovered after his death. It said that the truth of the Blackbottle Rock story was hidden within in the rug. You see, Trewin knew the rug would always be there because it was in a room where Cornelius, guilt burning in his heart, placed pictures of the dead and other things connected with them as a kind of secret memorial. He stipulated in his will that everything be preserved just as it was for as long as his family owned the house. When it was sold a few years ago, I persuaded the new owners to keep the attic locked up. I knew Sue would eventually stumble on the truth, so I decided I had to act…'

'What do you intend to do now, sir?' Mohan asked.

Penhale rubbed a hand over his balding head and let out a weary breath. 'The truth has to come out, and it has to come from me.'

'But you could get into serious trouble – breaking into the church, stealing from a precious book,' Charlie said, barely able to believe that he was actually feeling sorry for the broken man he'd known as the Creep.

The little man straightened his back and lifted his chin. 'Well, then, it's a good lesson to you young people. Not that you'd ever do anything like that, I'm sure. But when you do, you have to be big enough and strong enough to own up and face the consequences. I shall hand myself in to the police first thing in the morning.'

'But Sue told me you're supposed to be unveiling the plaque to Cornelius Penhale then,' Charlie pointed out.

Henry Penhale caught his breath for a moment. He had clearly forgotten about that. 'Well…that will have to be cancelled, the plaque destroyed.'

'Not necessarily,' Wei-Li piped up. 'Why don't you let the story come out a bit at a time rather than shock everyone – especially the locals who think of Cornelius as a hero. You could "stumble" on a clue here, a clue there, giving people time to get used to the idea that there's more to the story.'

'But what about his criminal activities?' Mohan demanded.

Henry Penhale smiled again. 'Your friend likes to speak plainly, doesn't he?'

'That's one way of describing it,' Wei-Li sighed. 'But I don't see any reason why anyone should know about that. What good would it do now? Return the page – secretly if you like.'

'Yes – and make some sort of donation to the church to cover the cost of repairs,' Charlie added.

'That would be quite wrong,' Mohan announced. 'And legally speaking, I believe it would make us accessories to a crime. I'll google it to confirm my suspicions, but—'

Charlie and Wei-Li's combined glares made him fall silent.

A few minutes later, they all trooped out of Rosebud Cottage for what Charlie knew would be the last time. The back edges of the storm clouds were sailing away over the distant hills, where cosy yellow house lights dotted the darkness on the Fowey side of the river. It felt good to feel the cool night air on his face – and to know that he and Fowey Paranormal Investigations had completed their mission.

*

'And so it gives me great pleasure to unveil this long-overdue plaque,' declared Henry Penhale to the small collection of locals and curious tourists gathered by the quay wall. The plaque itself was covered by a little purple curtain, and Penhale's hand lightly held a thin cord, ready to reveal it to the world. Charlie thought he was enjoying the limelight again, almost like his old self – but maybe not so irritatingly haughty.

Then Penhale let go of the cord for a moment. 'But before I do, I should mention that in the course of my researches, I've unearthed new information about what happened on that fateful day in 1856. There is still more to do, but for now suffice it to say it's become clear that Cornelius Penhale's role was not nearly as heroic as I had once thought. As his descendant, you can imagine my disappointment!'

There was some half-hearted chuckling at this attempted joke. Penhale grasped the cord once again.

'What I can say is that this is a story about tragedy and promising lives cut short, not heroism. So I now proudly reveal a new version of this memorial – to the victims of Polruan's Blackbottle Rock disaster.'

He pulled the cord and the curtain swept back exposing a shiny blue rectangle listing the names of all those who lost their lives. Charlie saw there was no mention of Cornelius Penhale on it at all. Polite applause echoed round the harbour, and then the crowd rapidly melted away to get on with their day. A local reporter approached Penhale with his notebook at the ready.

'Well,' said Sue as they wandered back to their cottage. 'I'm not sure what all that was about, but it's been a worthwhile trip. I've gathered more than enough information to make it into a good story.'

'I've got a better one,' Charlie said half under his breath.

She smiled wryly. 'I'm sure you have. But I'm writing a local history, not a ghost story!'

'Eh?' Dad frowned.

'Didn't you know Polruan was haunted?' Sue asked innocently.

'As in *spooks*?'

'Lots of 'em,' Charlie informed him.

'Yeah, right.'

Sue grinned knowingly at Charlie and reached out her hand. He hesitated for a moment, then grasped it, and she pulled him closer and turned it into a hug.

'Well done, Charlie.'

Looking over Sue's shoulder while he was still in her warm embrace, Charlie thought he saw Dad dab at the corner of his eye with his handkerchief. Maybe he had something in it…

seventeen

The car was all packed and ready to go. It was early Saturday morning, and the gentle light of the rising sun bathed the river and the green hills all around it. The pastel-coloured houses lining the Fowey side gleamed softly, and one window, catching the sun at just the right angle, reflected back a light so bright and dazzling that Charlie couldn't look at it. A black cormorant skimmed low and fast over the river towards the sea, and a crab boat making an early start followed at its own sedate pace. At first, the only sounds he could hear were the cries of the gulls and the symphony of clinking masts of the many boats anchored in the river. Then, ringing around the valley, came the chimes of the Fowey church clock marking the hour. This was followed by another familiar sound – the distant throb of a boat's engine. Charlie soon picked out the familiar orange and white Polruan ferry making its first return trip of the day from Fowey, leaving ripples expanding in its wake across the mirror-like surface.

'That's them!' Charlie ran to the railings at the top of the steps. But as the ferry drew closer, instead of seeing his friends looking out for him from the side of the boat as he had expected, he spotted Wei-Li, Mohan and two other passengers leaning over at the stern with their backs to him, gazing into the water. Even the ferryman kept glancing back over his shoulder as he steered. When the ferry was within twenty metres of the quay, Charlie was joined by Dad and Sue, and it was his father who spotted it.

'*Dolphin*!'

'Are you sure?' Sue asked.

Then Charlie saw it for himself – a triangular shark-like fin, cutting effortlessly through the water as the creature kept pace with the chugging vessel. He could make out its dark, sinuous shape just below the surface – and it was huge. Probably half as long as the boat itself. It twisted and turned playfully, easily darting from one side of the ferry to the other. Wei-Li was trailing a hand in the water and calling softly to the magnificent creature. Charlie broke into a smile. Knowing her, she was probably communicating with it.

The boat's engine note changed as the ferryman momentarily put it into reverse, bringing the boat to a halt by the steps. But no one disembarked. They were all still watching, as if mesmerised by the grace and beauty of the dolphin frolicking in the water: twisting, diving, occasionally breaking the surface and blowing like a whale. The ferryman and the few locals who were up and about were also captivated, so Charlie knew this must be a special moment even for a community like this one whose life revolved around the river and sea. Sue was taking pictures on her mobile. She had a nice, warm smile, Charlie noticed.

And then, after a few minutes of fun, the dolphin dived deeply and this time didn't reappear. The show was over, and Wei-Li and Mohan hopped off the ferry, which set off back to Fowey. Charlie thought for a moment that Wei-Li was wearing her Tai Chi costume, but then he saw it was more like a traditional Chinese outfit: a baggy-sleeved, shiny, silken dress with matching trousers in a rich, vivid blue with an elegant pink cherry blossom pattern. She had her gleaming black hair done up in some fancy way, with a little red flower fastened into it. He had to force himself not to stare. But although Charlie didn't possess Wei-Li's psychic powers, he somehow knew she had put on her special clothes today just for him…

'So,' said Dad, 'I finally get to meet the famous FPI!'

Mohan stepped forward and handed him a little card. 'We are at your service, sir, should you ever experience any strange events.'

'I'm afraid the strangest event I believe in is the way Charlie's bedroom can look as if it's been ransacked by burglars two hours after it's been tidied up.'

Charlie blushed, stealing a glance at Wei-Li.

'I wonder how long it will take him to let the whole story out,' mused Sue, looking back at the Beachcomber gift shop.

'Maybe it will never *all* come out...' Charlie couldn't help commenting.

'But the parts that really matter will,' said Wei-Li.

Dad frowned. 'You *are* a mysterious bunch! Why do I get the impression I'm an outsider?'

'Because you're a *non-believer*,' Charlie replied in a spooky voice.

'So you really are officially ghost hunters?" Sue asked Wei-Li.

'Ghost helpers. Mostly they are just confused, not even aware that they've died, and only in need of a little assistance to be released.'

'Or they're just recordings,' Mohan added. 'The ferry's coming back. We have to go. Goodbye, Charlie.' He offered his hand and there was a rather awkward, formal handshake.

Charlie turned to Wei-Li, and her unfathomable dark eyes held his for a heart-melting moment. Then she ran up and threw her slender arms around him, kissing him gently on the cheek.

'I hope we can stay in touch.'

There was a fragrance. Charlie didn't know much about things like that – could have been perfume, shampoo or under-arm deodorant for all he cared. He just knew it was the scent of heaven, and that he would never forget it.

'Yes. I'd like that.'

'Told you she fancied him,' Charlie heard Dad remark to Sue in a theatrical stage whisper. He felt his cheeks flushing, but he didn't care about that either.

Finally and reluctantly, Charlie made for the car. They had solved the Blackbottle mystery. The spirits were at peace – and maybe not just those of the Blackbottle Disaster, he thought as he glanced at Sue.

It was over. Time for a new beginning.

*

The engine of the fully laden old car complained as it laboured up Fore Street and out of Polruan.

'…And I'm sorry if it wasn't your cup of tea, Chas,' Dad was saying. 'I promise *you* can choose next year's holiday destination. Any ideas, mate?'

Sue twisted round, looking for Charlie's reaction. She was smiling. She understood.

Then he turned too, a last look back down the hill. In the gap between the cottages he could see the orange ferry chugging through the sparkling blue waters of the river, carrying Mohan and Wei-Li back to Fowey.

'Yep. I know *exactly* where.'

OUR STREET BOOKS

JUVENILE FICTION, NON-FICTION, PARENTING

Our Street Books are for children of all ages, delivering a potent mix of fantastic, rip-roaring adventure and fantasy stories to excite the imagination; spiritual fiction to help the mind and the heart; humorous stories to make the funny bone grow; historical tales to evolve interest; and all manner of subjects that stretch imagination, grab attention, inform, inspire and keep the pages turning. Our subjects include Non-fiction and Fiction, Fantasy and Science Fiction, Religious, Spiritual, Historical, Adventure, Social Issues, Humour, Folk Tales and more.

If you have enjoyed this book, why not tell other readers by posting a review on your preferred book site. Recent bestsellers from Our Street Books are:

Relax Kids: Aladdin's Magic Carpet

Marneta Viegas

Let Snow White, the Wizard of Oz and other fairytale characters show you and your child how to meditate and relax.

Meditations for young children aged 5 and up.

Paperback: 978-1-78279-869-9 Hardcover: 978-1-90381-666-0

Wonderful Earth

An interactive book for hours of fun learning

Mick Inkpen, Nick Butterworth

An interactive Creation story: Lift the flap, turn the wheel, look in the mirror, and more.

Hardcover: 978-1-84694-314-0

Boring Bible: Super Son Series 1
Andy Robb
Find out about angels, sin and the Super Son of God.
Paperback: 978-1-84694-386-7

Jonah and the Last Great Dragon
Legend of the Heart Eaters
M.E. Holley
When legendary creatures invade our world, only dragon-fire can destroy them; and Jonah alone can control the Great Dragon.
Paperback: 978-1-78099-541-0 ebook: 978-1-78099-542-7

Little Prayers Series: Classic Children's Prayers
Alan and Linda Parry
Traditional prayers told by your child's favourite creatures.
Hardcover: 978-1-84694-449-9

Magnificent Me, Magnificent You The Grand Canyon
Dawattie Basdeo, Angela Cutler
A treasure filled story of discovery with a range of inspiring fun exercises, activities, songs and games for children aged 6 to 11.
Paperback: 978-1-78279-819-4

Q is for Question
An ABC of Philosophy
Tiffany Poirier
An illustrated non-fiction philosophy book to help children aged 8 to 11 discover, debate and articulate thought-provoking, open-ended questions about existence, free will and happiness.
Hardcover: 978-1-84694-183-2

Relax Kids: How to be Happy
52 positive activities for children
Marneta Viegas
Fun activities to bring the family together.
Paperback: 978-1-78279-162-1

Rise of the Shadow Stealers
The Firebird Chronicles
Daniel Ingram-Brown
Memories are going missing. Can Fletcher and Scoop unearth their own lost history and save the Storyteller's treasure from the shadows?
Paperback: 978-1-78099-694-3 ebook: 978-1-78099-693-6

Readers of ebooks can buy or view any of these bestsellers by clicking on the live link in the title. Most titles are published in paperback and as an ebook. Paperbacks are available in traditional bookshops. Both print and ebook formats are available online.

Find more titles and sign up to our readers' newsletter at
http://www.johnhuntpublishing.com/children-and-young-adult
Follow us on Facebook at
https://www.facebook.com/JHPChildren and Twitter at
https://twitter.com/JHPChildren